# PRAISE FO

B0203006986     04/2022

W9-BIV-692

West Palm Beach, FL ...406-4...98

"Carley Moore's voice is a nec...
With each of her works, her ...
wider—*Panpocalypse* is a mast.... ... ....
the intricacies of our bodies and our minds, the city and the state, with fearless passion and bold, political intelligence. We need this book right now, and we'll need it in all the nows to come."

**—MICHELLE TEA, author of *Against Memoir***

"Here's the sexy, sad, queer, disabled, time-bending romp through the bleak pandemic landscape that you've been waiting for! No one lays herself as bare on the page as Carley Moore, and *Panpocalypse* is her most naked work to date. Whoever you are, and wherever you need your bike to take you, this book will speak to the universal need for love, touch, and acceptance in the hardest of times."

**—LYNN MELNICK, author of *Refusenik***

"Carley Moore's stunning novel captures the haunted dreams of our present world and the dire imaginings of an uncertain future. Moore tells a story of queer longing that moves between past and present, imagination and memory, all the while taking pleasure and grief and hope by the hand and bringing them along as a mooring against social decay. This is a powerful story, naked and mournful, but also sharp and sensual and playful. It's a book that will linger with you for weeks and months and years."

**—JAMES POLCHIN, author of *Indecent Advances***

"I couldn't put this book down. The prose crackles, the story line shimmers; it has the energy of a queer, disabled Elena Ferrante living in modern-day New York City. There's gritty reality, and there's also the most fun escapist fantasy (and time travel!). *Panpocalypse* is a must-read for anyone who has yearned for connection in quarantined times."

**—AMY SHEARN, author of *Unseen City***

"*Panpocalypse* is a rousing, eerily enchanting, and verve-filled exploration of love and life in the midst of brittle collapse and upheaval. Moore's sharp and provocative voice adds much-needed complexity to the public discourse about the impact of COVID-19 on queer and disabled communities."

**—JAMIA WILSON, author of *This Book Is Feminist***

# PANPOCALYPSE

PANSEXUAL + PANDEMIC + APOCALYPSE = PANPOCALYPSE

## CARLEY MOORE

**THE FEMINIST PRESS**
AT THE CITY UNIVERSITY OF NEW YORK
**NEW YORK CITY**

Published in 2022 by the Feminist Press
at the City University of New York
The Graduate Center
365 Fifth Avenue, Suite 5406
New York, NY 10016
feministpress.org

First Feminist Press edition 2022

Copyright © 2022 by Carley Moore
All rights reserved.

This book was made possible thanks to a grant from
New York State Council on the Arts with the support
of the Governor and the New York State Legislature.

**ART WORKS.**
arts.gov

This book is supported in part by an award from
the National Endowment for the Arts.

No part of this book may be reproduced, used, or stored in any information
retrieval system or transmitted in any form or by any means, electronic, mechanical,
photocopying, recording, or otherwise, without prior written permission from
the Feminist Press at the City University of New York, except in the case of brief
quotations embodied in critical articles and reviews.

First printing March 2022

Cover design by Suki Boynton
Text design by Drew Stevens

Library of Congress Cataloging-in-Publication Data

Names: Moore, Carley, author.
Title: Panpocalypse / Carley Moore.
Description: New York : Feminist Press, 2022.
Identifiers: LCCN 2021041178 (print) | LCCN 2021041179 (ebook) | ISBN
  9781952177606 (paperback) | ISBN 9781952177026 (ebook)
Subjects: LCSH: Moore, Carley. | People with disabilities—Fiction. |
  COVID-19 (Disease)—Fiction. | Lesbians—Fiction. | New York
  (N.Y.)—Fiction. | LCGFT: Autobiographical fiction.
Classification: LCC PS3613.O55454 P36 2022  (print) | LCC PS3613.O55454
  (ebook) | DDC 813/.6—dc23
LC record available at https://lccn.loc.gov/2021041178
LC ebook record available at https://lccn.loc.gov/2021041179

PRINTED IN THE UNITED STATES OF AMERICA

*For my mom*

# PART 1

# PANPOCALYPSE

The following chapters were published weekly online
during the COVID-19 pandemic
in New York City in the summer of 2020.

*WEEK ONE*
*MAY 3, 2020*

# ROBOT DICTATOR

*Hi, this is a test. How do you like my voice?*

This is a work of autofiction; some things are true, some things are made up. I am currently making this as you are reading it, and because of my various disabilities, I'm dictating it.

I think it's going to work.

*Robot dictation device, robot dictator, if you can learn my voice, if you can fix my mistakes, then we can write this book together.*

*Good little robot, good little dog, good little machine. Would you like us to give you a name? What do you want to be called?*

Capitalize delete backspace backspace backspace.

*I don't know what to call you yet, so let's see what happens. Little robot, I need you because of my muscles. Because the pain in my shoulder and my hips doesn't go away. It's worse during the pandemic, but everything is worse during the pandemic.*

This is a weekly gift should you need it. I make it for us both so that we don't go crazy, but honestly I'm already mentally ill. It's for the community, because now more than ever we must make our own things and take care of ourselves as best we can. Let me know if you think of a name for my dictation robot.

Sometimes the robot breaks and can't hear me, and I get fed up and type and hurt my muscles anyway, because that's what we do—we work through pain. So you may experience disjointedness or breaks or spasms in the text and in me. They can't be helped. Kids always used to call me a spaz when they wanted to fuck with me, and I'm reclaiming it. They weren't wrong, they were just assholes.

Disjointed time, broken time, nonlinear time, lockdown time, sick time—I aim to fuck with time because mass illness has fucked time. We're all disabled now.

# MY BIKE

I buy a bike. A store in the East Village is open for essential workers of the pandemic—delivery people on bikes, mostly immigrants, often undocumented. In line with me, there's a man with a broken bike chain and two friends with a bike that needs new brakes.

A couple homeless men wander by. "What are you waiting for?"

"Bike shop," we mumble through our masks.

There's a light drizzle. I fold and unfold my umbrella. It's a gray day, not a riding day.

A man in a motorized wheelchair zips up too close to me so that he can ask if the tobacco store next to the bike shop is closed.

"I think so, looks like it," I say through my purple bandanna mask with raccoons on it. My friend sent it to me. She's with her wife uptown in the Bronx, where they live now. I miss her but can't see her. I can't see any of my friends, and I'm single and clinically depressed so I cry a lot. I have a few casual lovers, but I can't get to them. I miss touch. Sometimes I feel abandoned by my friends. Friends who made queer germ circles without me, friends who left the city for country houses, friends who are married or coupled. I feel unitless, adrift on the waves of my own tears.

The man in the wheelchair speeds away and into the bike lane without replying. I love how fast people in motorized wheelchairs go, how many more I've seen in the street since lockdown, alongside bikes, taking up the middle of the road. I like seeing people in wheelchairs in the middle of Second Avenue. It's a glorious "fuck you" to the walking. A middle finger to the abled city, the not-sick city. The whole city is quarantined now.

My parents never got me a wheelchair, though in those last few years when things were really bad, I would have been better off with one. But maybe I didn't want one. Maybe I was steeped in my own shame and refused one.

Inside the bike shop, a man in his late twenties or early thirties helps me. I called ahead to see whether they had a bike for me, and they did. He's kind, sweet, and wears a green-and-yellow mask. I wonder if his partner made it for him.

I say, "I have a disability so my balance isn't always great, but I can ride, though it's been a while. I need to be able to touch the ground with my feet when I stop, and I need a cruiser with a wide seat and maybe more than three gears. I want baskets for groceries, and a color would be great."

"I think I have a good bike for you." He's a total professional, not a bike-bro dick. He goes to the back and then wheels out my bike. She's magenta, low, with cream-colored rims on fat-tire wheels. "It's a step-through so you can get on and off easily. Really light too."

We pick out my seat and have an honest conversation about my ass. Maybe our masks make it easier for us to do this.

"Some of us get very sweaty and some of us don't," he says. "It's just about bodies and where your sit bones are located."

"I get really sweaty and my butt is big."

"Got it." He shows me the widest, softest seat. I am also thinking about my pussy, and that she needs me to take care of her. More than anything, I want to feel good on this bike and I want to connect with her. I need endorphins because the pandemic has made me so depressed I'm afraid I'm going to have another breakdown.

We pick out locks, the baskets, a helmet. I choose the ventilated one over the cuter, more old-school one because I know how sweaty my head and face get.

I max out a credit card to buy her. I am a master at maxing out a credit card, paying it down little by little, and then maxing it out again in a moment of desperation and/or longing.

My bike guy seems excited for me. "I'll call you. It'll be ready tomorrow."

I'm numb when I leave, panicked about the money. I am waiting for my stimulus check, which I've already decided to give away, but there is suffering in the world and I have bought an object.

# FIRST RIDE

We're almost two months into the pandemic. The day I pick up my bike, it's sunny and I'm sweating. At lights I stop. I stick to the bike lanes mostly and just pedal. My leg muscles tingle and my heart beats harder in my chest than it has since the lockdown began. Before I really know what I'm doing, I'm at the mouth of the Williamsburg Bridge. I stare up at the incline. Can I do it? Should I try? I take a picture of it with my phone and text my friend and ex-husband, Guapo, that I'm going to try. He knows my disability better than anyone, except maybe my mom.

"Do it!" he texts back.

The incline is long but not steep. I pass walkers and shift gears. When bikes pass me, I'm pulled toward them like I'm on some invisible puppet string. I will have to think about this, but I don't stop. My legs burn and I switch gears. Panting, but riding. Going, going, gone.

What if I never go back to Manhattan?

What if I stay in Brooklyn with my friends?

What if I find a secret bar where people are allowed to touch?

At the crest of the bridge, I wave and talk to the river. "Hi, East River. Hi, garbage barge. I love you." I count masks and remember that bikers are queer and cute, at least the ones coming at me from Brooklyn. Black bandanna mask. Black cutoff jean shorts. Rainbow flag mask. Mullet and red bandanna. Black mask. Black mask. No mask. No mask. No mask. The Citi Bikers have fewer masks, are taller and white. Straight men and their tall women. *Nothing can touch us*, their maskless faces say. Orthodox women and their teenage daughters walking, never riding, maskless.

My muscles burn and I get off to rest at a little inlet on the bridge before the decline into Brooklyn. I'm almost to the other side, where nothing is open, and no one can see me. My heart keeps pounding out of my chest. I'm happy. For once, in the last two months of depression, anxiety, and worry, I feel joy.

There are two women on roller skates in the inlet. Their skates are gold and they wear hot pants and crop tops. One says to the other, "Got it, go!" and starts to film her. The starlet waggles her tongue at the camera and shoots the duck, pumping her leg to keep herself moving. I smile at them through my mask, but they can't see. I keep forgetting that no one can see my mouth and nose, no one can see my expressions. I have walked this city for twenty-five years full of expressions. I have smiled, frowned, laughed, and yelled, and now I am faceless.

*You are so pretty!* I want to shout at them, but I don't because I don't want to bother them and I don't remember how to speak in public.

I keep riding down the slope of the bridge and into Brooklyn.

When I get home a few hours later, I look at the queer, sad, desperate, lonely dating app, Lex. This isn't an insult. It's just how it is for single queers right now, or maybe since the beginning of queers. Longing all around.

A new post, an unlinked-to-anybody account. No pics. *Are you lonely? Do you want to fuck and be fucked? Do you want to touch each other underground like they did in Paris at Le Monocle in the 1930s? Shhh . . . it's against the law.*

I type a quick message into the ether: "Yes, but how?"

In the morning when I check my phone, the ad is gone, but there's a message. "We'll find you."

# A BRIEF HISTORY OF BIKES

My first bike is beautiful. A sparkly green Schwinn with a cream-colored banana seat, tall handlebars, and white streamers. I love that bike, but learning how to ride it is an early confrontation with the fact that something is wrong with me.

My father takes off the training wheels, runs alongside me, and lets go, like you see in the movies. Except I fall. Again and again. We try on the sidewalk, in the street, in parking lots, over and over again, in every corner of this small, dying Rust Belt town. We try for two years. I fall so many times my knees and shins are perpetually scabbed. I eat gravel and my dad pulls it out of my bottom lip with tweezers. My mom puts peroxide on my wounds and I listen to my skin sizzle and bubble, crying and wincing.

The neighborhood is either rooting for me or against me. I can't tell, but I'm definitely a watched object. My parents and I wonder out loud if I can do it, can I learn how to ride a bike? At that point, we don't know what's wrong with me. There is a long search. One doctor says cerebral palsy, but my parents don't believe him and they're right not to. But for the longest time, I am a mystery. I can do a lot in the morning and very little at night. It's totally weird, even to me. Two years pass.

I finally learn to balance. My mom and I are on the track at the local community college. She's wearing an orange sweatshirt. My dad jogs slowly. My brother zips along on his bike. He's three years younger but learned to ride in a day. I hate him for that, for not having what I have, for being well and fit, my parents' dream child.

My mom holds on to the bike seat, gives me a push, and lets go. For the first time in two years, I don't fall. My body finally understands the bike, or feels the center of gravity, or something. I'm stunned. The joy I feel as I take off cancels out that hate. I leave them all behind as I circle the track. I pass my father, who is cheering. My mom jumps up and down. The wind blows through my bowl cut. I'm free. I can leave them behind, but I don't yet. They are watching me and it feels good.

Somebody steals my green Schwinn. I park her on the side of my house, near the kitchen window. I'm in a hurry because I have to pee, so I don't put her in the garage. In the morning I sob when I find out she's missing. We drive around the neighborhood looking for the person who took her. My father is livid. He has a thing about our stuff, our lack of respect for the objects he buys us.

"You have to learn your lesson. If you won't take care of your things, who will?"

My mom can't help me because my dad has already decided my punishment. "You'll have to save your allowance," she says, and hugs me.

Sometimes, when my parents fight about how dirty the house is, he relents and agrees to help clean. My mom leaves to go to the mall to get a much-needed break, and my dad yells, "If you don't pick up your fucking toys in an hour, they're all going in the garbage!"

It works, but I cry as he dangles my Barbies over the trash chute. I understand that I'm not allowed to break and lose my things, but he is.

Eventually I get a shitty orange-and-yellow bike from Kmart. The name, Prairie Flower, is stenciled on her frame. She sucks, but I ride her anyway and pretend to my friends that she's amazing, even though her chain falls off whenever I pick up speed.

In high school I get a cream cruiser with a brown seat. At some point my brother steals this bike from me and sells it. My parents don't believe me, but he confesses it to me in the family room, where we keep and tell our secrets. It's also where he gets wasted and I let two boys fingerfuck me so I can wear a tampon. I have a clear goal and I need their willpower to break my hymen. Boys aren't difficult like girls—they're always willing.

College for me is bikeless. I take the bus except for one time when I ride my roommate's ten-speed in the middle of the night because her boyfriend sits on my bed and won't leave. The rest of the house is asleep. I say I have my period and he lets me go. The tires are totally flat, but I keep going until I break the rims. I pass the dark cemetery and pray he's not following me. The seat hurts my crotch and I can't maneuver the curved handlebars. I make it to my boyfriend's house just as the sun is coming up. He's trying to break up with me and has banned me from his apartment but lets me in because I'm so scared.

For a long time I associate bikes with boys. My boyfriend in my twenties, the first man I thought I would marry, is a cyclist, Austrian, austere about food and exercise. I am my usual chubby self and still at war with my body about exercise, which I find shameful and disgusting. We live in New York and I'm in awe of the subway, so I don't understand why anyone would choose to bike when we can take this marvelous, disgusting, fascinating system of tunnels anywhere we want to go.

"You're always riding away from me," I tell him. He never officially dumps me but increasingly removes himself from my life until I'm living alone in a sublet where I get robbed and mugged in the same week.

In my thirties my husband, Guapo, and I buy bikes together. He cajoles me into riding. This is before the city has bike lanes, and speeding trucks and cars rattle me. I'm out of shape and the big hill in the Prospect Park loop feels like a defeat to me. When we separate, we sell our bikes. Aside from one terrifying ride on a Citi Bike, I don't bike again for six years.

# DOPAMINE

I still struggle with how to describe it and what to call it. The technical name is long and needs repeating. People sometimes like to write it down. It's not something even your average neurologist has heard of. *It's a movement disorder. One in two million people have it. I don't make enough dopamine, so I take synthetic dopamine. I do okay now.* That's what I say if I don't want to talk about it, or I don't know you.

If I feel open to you, I might say, *I couldn't walk very well until I was eleven.* I might say, *I was very sick.* I hardly ever say, *I wanted to kill myself I was in so much pain* or, *I made a plan for how I might do it.* If we eat a meal together, I will say, *I take a lot of medication,* so you know I'm not just popping pills. The hardest of all to say is, *I am sometimes in a lot of pain,* because then people want me to describe the pain. It's a tender gesture, but it takes so much effort to describe pain. *My muscles are tight,* I might offer to get people to stop asking, because pain isn't describable. It is there or it isn't. If you are not in pain, you can forget what it feels like. If you are in pain, it colors and shapes everything.

As I write this, I have a terrible headache. I am hoping it will go away because I took my medicine.

When I buy my new magenta bike, I'm in pain. Pain decides to buy a bike. Pain wants an escape. Pain doesn't give a fuck about money. Pain will spend your money. The wonderful essayist Sonya Huber titled her essay collection *Pain Woman Takes Your Keys.* Damn, is she right about that. A pain woman is not rational. She takes what she needs.

*WEEK TWO*
*MAY 10, 2020*

# GRAY RIDE

I ride because I have nothing else to do, and I want to push the city's loneliness up against my own.

It's late when I get on my bike. Windy. The streets are empty except for delivery workers and the occasional Citi Biker. I notice the same tall, white male Citi Bikers who ride next to each other while talking, and who gesticulate with their hands. They are so well-balanced, they don't need to hold the handlebars. The confidence of it is a little galling, but I aspire to have that level of balance, to not be such a spaz.

I circle the park then head west. Per usual, I mostly follow the bike lanes because I feel safest there. I want to go up Hudson, the wide expanse of it. I stop at lights and think about my ex-girlfriend Eurydice, whom I dated for six months, the first woman I fell in love with. She is a bike messenger, a former volleyball player, a poet, and a mother of three children her ex will not let her see. Often broke. Gorgeous. Angry and sweet. She said her favorite thing about riding in the city was whizzing past construction workers as they whistled at her.

Her name is Eurydice because I am that little bitch Orpheus who can't stop herself from looking backward and ruining everything. I am not above seduction via the lute. Poets, you know.

At a light on Christopher and Hudson, pulled up against the curb and resting my ass on my seat more comfortably than I thought possible, I text her, "I got a bike!"

"Bikes are cool. Be careful," she texts back.

"Are you delivering? I thought maybe we could meet up."

"No. Working at home." She told me a couple weeks ago that she got a job processing bankruptcy claims.

"I miss you. I wonder if we can be friends?" I ask.

"Stay safe," she sends back. She doesn't give me much; she did for a little bit and then it all blew up.

I'm off again, trying to ride through the shame I feel at reaching out, the futility of it. The bike lane on Hudson is painted light green like a faded tennis court. The pink leaves of the magnolia trees have collected in the gutter. My face, especially around my mouth, sweats into my mask. My heart beats faster than it ever does in yoga.

I continue up Hudson and over toward the Whitney. The wind picks up and I pedal harder to keep going. For a moment, the wind is so strong that I pedal and don't move. I tip over and panic for a second, but I'm okay. I get up.

In this moment, I name my bike Lana, after my favorite Frank O'Hara poem: "Poem [Lana Turner has collapsed!]" I write about this poem often, how it's become a kind of disability theme song for me. I like imagining myself as Lana Turner, collapsing on the sidewalk in epic Hollywood style, instead of my usual graceless catastrophes. In January I fell on the street and broke my arm. From research, I know that Lana Turner collapsed from exhaustion, but she did eventually get back up, after some rest at the hospital. The studios pushed her too hard.

I pass the old awnings of what used to be the meatpacking plants and then queer clubs in the '80s and '90s. I never went to those clubs, but I wish I had. I still want to go to a dungeon. I want to tie someone up and fuck them and get dragged around on a leash.

I stop again to take pictures of a potted tree that's fallen over. A man in a flannel jacket with a little dog walks past the fallen tree. The dog sniffs and pulls at its leash to stay. I push off.

I'm getting used to my bike's stopping and starting, the way I can land my foot on the curb and sit on the seat like I'm riding a horse with a saddle. Sometimes I hop off the seat and sometimes I stay on it. Later when I get home, I feel the inside of my right knee bruising from where I hit the bar when I hop off. I make a note to myself to work on that, to ease off my bike more gently. I turn south along a brick street that's been sanded smooth by construction and traffic. There are no cars anywhere. Underneath the High Line, I pause to take a video of a clutch of vines hanging off the steel railroad tracks. The vines undulate like waves in the wind. A man on the stairs looks down at me and away.

I remember Eurydice, when we first started dating. We are in Red Hook at a bar full of dykes who don't know what to make of us. We kiss against the wall. She presses hard into me. We have to go home so we can fuck. But she has her bike, and in a moment of panic outside the bar, I get on the bus without her. I think she's behind me, but the door closes as the bus driver tells her she can't take her bike on the bus and then we take off without her.

I want to cry. The bus passengers stare at me. Have they never seen a couple like us? I am at times ashamed of our age difference. I know I am too old for her, but she's also been through so much. She's more jaded than me. I am the hopeful, stupid one who doesn't understand how the world works, according to her.

I sit down defeated and space out. And then I see her out the window, pedaling alongside the bus, stopping when we stop, moving when we move, keeping her eye on me. My heart beats in my pussy. The passengers soften to us, an old lady smiles at me and nods. We're in a rom-com for a minute and the city decides to play along. I blush.

I have never seen a rom-com about a middle-aged, bisexual, disabled cis woman and her trans girlfriend.

# PINK BRIDGE

Once, when my mom visits me, we walk across the Williamsburg Bridge. Often when she visits, I am torn between caring for her and caring for my kid. But this is a good day. My mother has agreed to walk to Brooklyn. She's not afraid of the city like she sometimes is. She walks next to me instead of scurrying ahead or behind and saying "Where to?" on every corner, which annoys me and makes me feel like a tour guide.

The women in my family are prone to darting and hiding, like mice, like we're not safe, like we're in a maze and about to get caught. It's May, we've survived Mother's Day without a fight, and it's warm but not hot, and sunny with a full blue sky. We link arms, the subway cars rattle and roll beneath us. We laugh and talk about books. I can tease her, and she doesn't mind because I'm not being a bitch this weekend. I am nice.

"Why did they paint it pink?" she asks.

"I don't know, but it's such a good color." For most of my adult life, I confuse the bridges and don't know their descending order from Harlem to the Statue of Liberty.

I might even say, *We're on the Manhattan Bridge*, and think I'm right and she'll agree, because we are two country mice, one who ran away to the city and one who ran away and came back to the country.

I allow her to complain about my stepfather, to tell me things I don't want to know. Newly divorced, I am not yet tired of dating. I still like men as lovers. I am in love with a new man, and he's opened me up sexually and taught me that I like to tie him up and punish him. Hurting him in this dom way makes me cackle with delight. My boots land on the bridge's walkway and my dress blows in the wind.

When we get off the bridge, I take her to a taco place I love, La Superior. We get margaritas and tacos and guacamole. The alcohol loosens my tongue, and I tell her about my new boyfriend and that I am happy. I don't tell her about domming and subbing.

"Are you okay?" she asks.

"Mommy, I really am," I say.

I don't tell her about the last time I was here: two years ago with my friend Guitar, right before my marriage ended. I was talking about a forbidden crush, Pony, and I burst into tears because I felt such shame about my longing.

In the bathroom, I looked at myself in the mirror. What did I see? A woman with the wrong haircut. A trapped woman. A woman with animal hungers. A crying woman who was in love with her therapist and Pony and a student who lingered during office hours and reminded her of JFK.

You are married, I told myself. You must make this work, even if you are unhappy. I can't remember what Guitar said, but I know it was something good and scary. She helped me leave my marriage. She was hard and pushed me. I didn't like it, but she was a prophet that way. She took me out, showed me around, and let me see that at night I could do things. There were parties and men who wanted me, even if only for a night.

"Are you really okay?" my mom pushes.

"Mommy, I promise, yes."

I only call her Mommy when I am very happy or very sad.

# TINY TIM IS MY AVATAR

The best version of *A Christmas Carol* is the Disney one with Mickey Mouse as Bob Cratchit and Scrooge McDuck as Ebenezer Scrooge. The cutest disabled cartoon character ever is Tiny Tim, drawn as a small Mickey Mouse, with a stick for a crutch.

I watch *Mickey's Christmas Carol* on the gold shag carpet of the split-level ranch house we move to when I am ten. I'm twelve when the movie airs on NBC during prime time. This is the era of thirteen channels. My brother and I wear footie pajamas and sip glasses of pop. We are deep into all the Christmas shows of that era, but especially *Mickey's Christmas Carol, Rudolph the Red-Nosed Reindeer*, and *A Charlie Brown Christmas*. I'm drawn to Tiny Tim with turned-in legs and crutch (likely rickets and TB, though Dickens never says), Rudolph with his strange glowing nose and island of misfit toys, and Charlie Brown with his "blockheaded" ideas and sad excuse for a Christmas tree. If I am twelve, that means I have been diagnosed and "cured." I take a magic pill several times a day, synthetic dopamine, pure and uncut then, pink, round, and chalky. Most days it makes me queasy. Sometimes I throw it up, until I learn to eat something with it.

It's December 10, the snow in western New York is deep and heavy. My father builds a fire in the fireplace, which is special, because the exertion makes him testy. Like Bob Cratchit, my dad has been trying to make partner at his firm for years. It's the backdrop of much of my parents' conversation: money and how to have more of it. My brother and I are especially close at Christmas. We ask for a lot of presents, and we usually get them. We still believe in Santa and the transformational power of a holiday, even though our parents have awful fights around Christmas, usually about the tree. This year we have plans to catch Santa in the middle of the night. We have flashlights and an idea for a booby trap.

My mom is laid off this year from her secretary job and does needlepoint on the couch covered in an afghan. We want her to be a stay-at-home mom, but my dad is against that. We're not sure what my mom wants, and we probably don't care because we are kids.

I wonder what my parents think when we watch Tiny Tim. They are glad I did not die, though I won't know that until years later when they tell me that for a while they thought I had a fatal disease called Friedreich's ataxia, which often leads to death in the early twenties.

Like Tiny Tim, I am the sweetest cripple. A good girl. I submit to all the tests and the touching and poking and prodding. I learn early on to be the best patient, the cutest and most obedient. The one with the highest cartoon-pitch voice, because then the doctors will take care of me. It's not until much later in my life that I stop being good. It turns out, I am not afraid of much because I've been in so much pain for so long. I don't care. I can walk now, and later I will walk into so much trouble, simply because I can. Disabled people have a right to be bad too.

I joke with only my closest people that I am that little Tiny Tim, so cute, so twee, and so irresistible as to take over the whole story. Once Dickens—he is such a master at ripping our hearts out—stages Tiny Tim's funeral, we will do anything for that little sickie. He transforms the evil Scrooge because he's so gracious and good. "God bless us, every one," he says, and then he snuggles with Scrooge in a rocking chair. He's not a whiner. He's an inspiration.

I'd like to snuggle with that little Mickey Mouse Tiny Tim. I'd like to throw him up in the air and catch him. It matters that he doesn't have a little wheelchair, because that would render him culturally not cute, not curable, too disabled, and too distant for grabbing and touching. People love to touch the disabled and pregnant without consent. Tiny Tim is a disability doll. Floppy and compliant.

I call Gina, one of my casual lovers. I'm not allowed to see her during the pandemic. She's immunosuppressed and lives in New Jersey. I can't get to her and it's potentially dangerous that I see her. Though this gets old. I think we should pod up somehow. I do a lot of research on various germ pods and configurations. A recent article in the *Times* says, "Bubble size should not matter, researchers say, so long as the boundaries are firm. But, of course, with more people come more opportunities for leaks."

"Can you ask your doctor?" I ask. "Can you talk to your ex-wife?"

Gina's been saying no to me for a long time, but she's getting lonely too. We want to touch each other. I want to sit on her lap. She bought a new sex toy that is shaped like an *L* and looks like two dicks.

"Don't dig in. Don't be stubborn." I haven't seen anyone in two months except my kid, her dad, Guapo, and his girlfriend, Pauline.

"Okay, I will talk to them." Her ex is afraid too, doesn't want the kids to get sick. There's some New Jersey–commuter, New York City–phobia going on too, like if you escape from New York City every day, you are not obliged to take care of your city, to be with it.

"I want to be able to visit you and take care of you after your surgery. I don't want everyone to think I'm a stranger," I say.

"I want that too." We have talked about her pussy and the things we will be able to do with it. I am agnostic about genitals. I want you to have what's right for your gender. I work with everything. Sex toys to me are extensions of body parts if we want them to be. They are robots too or just useful and increasingly well-designed, cute tools. I like dicks and pussies just the same, though I have moods and preferences depending on the day. The sex for me just has to be queer, negotiated, playful, and intimate if we are ready. An asshole can be a pussy as easily as a dick. But sometimes a woman doesn't want to have her dick anymore and so it's time.

Tonight I go out on my bike at six p.m. I have heartburn, gas, a stomachache. I can't bear it anymore. "I can't do it," I text her. "I can't do it. I can't not touch another adult for this long. I can't."

I pedal up University Place, down Thirteenth, and up Sixth Avenue. Good bike lanes. No Citi Bikers at this hour, just me and the delivery men, who give me a lot of space, who are so much faster than I am.

I pass Trader Joe's. I miss their food, but I haven't been in lately. I shop the small, shitty grocery stores during this time. Gristedes. Morton Williams. Outside Trader Joe's, they've set up tables for people to pack their bags. It's not busy, but I can't figure out the system, so I don't stop. I hate food now anyways. All it does is hurt me and all I do is prepare it. I don't really deal with my IBS. Except to cut out gluten, sugar, and cow's milk, but even that's not working lately.

I fart my way up Sixth Avenue. Streaming farts, I consider riding up to Macy's but decide that's too depressing. I cut over to Seventh Avenue. I practice not hopping off my bike but stopping and leaning a little on my toes while keeping my ass on the seat. I'm doing a good job.

The clapping starts when I am on Hudson. Outside a bar that has takeout is a big crowd drinking beer out of plastic cups, kinda keeping away from one another, but not really. Chefs come out and bang pans. I stop and clap and clap and clap. People really love the clapping and I know it's important for essential workers, but I am not able to get caught up in it. I don't want to clap. I want doctors and nurses, some of whom are my former students, to have proper PPE. I want a president who isn't a racist rapist, and I want a cure. I want to touch people instead of clapping alone on my bike.

In the rabbit warren parts of the West Village, like Jane, Charles, and West Tenth, there are families on stoops playing cards. I'm jealous and I keep going, wondering why I don't have a family like this, a house like this, a stoop, a charming group of witty West Village neighbors.

Money probably. Self-isolation maybe. Class rage.

When I get home, I see a message on Lex. "Do you want to make a germ bubble with me?"

"Maybe," I write back.

# I RODE THE LOOP

"I will miss your selfhood still transmitting on screens," I tell my students. It's our last day and I manage to shower before class. My eyes are tired and squinty in the Zoom square that forces me to stare at my face for several hours on certain days. It's a mirror, I guess, but a live one, and so much more evil, like the queer mirror in *Snow White*. That mirror is a bitter queen. The Zoom mirror is too.

When we began the semester, we were physically together in a classroom, laughing, talking, and writing. The last day before spring break, I said that I'd see them in two weeks. We had no idea that, a year later, I still would not have seen them in person. I'd lowered my expectations for them but was hard on myself. I felt guilty that I couldn't teach them in the ways I wanted to—in person, in a shared physical space, with humor and care. I gave them the option of turning in a COVID-19 diary instead of our usual research essay, and many of them did. They were terrified and wanted to come back to the city. They wanted me to describe it for them, to tell them what it was like to be living in the epicenter of death. I often couldn't describe it, and felt I should spare them. Some were taking care of siblings and parents. They were rightfully angry at the ways the university had handled their leaving.

We do a lot of checking in, using a number system from one to ten, with the option to pass. One is awful. Ten is amazing. I often rate myself at a three or four. Even on their worst days, they say five or six. Zoom gives me migraines, and often after I teach for three or four hours I fall into a corpse-like sleep on the couch instantly. The fatigue is different from anything I've ever experienced, and I consider myself the master of exhaustion. I am grateful it's the last day. *The whole experiment needs to end*, I think. But I make a lesson plan and teach that day as best as I can.

During this last class, Gina finally texts me back. "No, it's too risky to see you," she writes. "My ex is worried I'll get sick and then she'll have to take care of the kids on her own." It's all valid, except I hate them both for controlling me, deciding my fate. I don't matter, I pout, and try not to cry through my last class.

My students and I listen to Rosa Alcalá's poem "You Rode a Loop." I say to them, "What do you think? Do some freewriting for five minutes about the loops in your life. Mental, physical, in your past, your present. Make sure to include one object like Rosa does." This morning on Twitter, an essayist I like said prompts are dangerous. Well, no. There are good prompts and bad prompts. I craft prompts very carefully. They need both constraints and openness.

In this last moment of listening, writing, and sharing in the Zoom classroom, I feel psychically linked to Rosa, who has become in recent years a dear friend to one of my best friends in graduate school, Jonna. In November, Rosa and Jonna hosted me at UTEP in celebration of my novel. I see a way forward in Zoom. It will be sonic rather than visual, more language, fewer screens.

In November, in El Paso, I am very happy. The events are well-attended and the community comes out for me, a stranger. Bill, who runs the bookstore there, is one of the sweetest booksellers I've ever met, and booksellers are already the sweetest. I travel with my kid, and she and Jonna's kids adore each other, like in a deep nerd, weird, loving way. We tell them they are like cousins and they go for it. Jonna and I hang out like we did in graduate school, but with better food and in the desert, which is one of my favorite landscapes, the wide blue sky, the heat and chill, the artistic pull of expanse and vista. We stay in a little adobe Craftsman, and every morning I walk down the street to eat at an amazing café with several gluten-free treats.

I read with Andrea Cote Botero, a Colombian poet who teaches in UTEP's bilingual MFA program. She reads in Spanish and then there's a translation. I miss reading with poets. My Spanish is rusty. I don't tell anyone about how happy I am in Spanish-speaking places. My grandma was Cuban and I was a Spanish minor and studied abroad in Spain, but this information feels irrelevant. I associate Spanish with my liberation, travel, understanding certain things

...at my family that have to do with mood, smells, jokes, and rumors.

After the reading, I drink mezcal with Andrea's husband. Rosa is next to me and we talk about a poet we both love. Jonna is on the other side, and I feel my worlds coming together, my graduate school life and my novelist life. My straight life and my queer life. Mostly I am happy to sit between two dear women-writers and friends, drink mezcal, and listen in on both Spanish and English. Andrea's husband has been visiting the migration camps in Juárez and talking to people who are waiting. He tells us about the Cuban sandwich vendors, how quickly they have made businesses to feed people. I am so grateful for this knowledge, firsthand and real, not filtered through white journalists. The border is not imaginary in El Paso, the border and the wall are there every day.

I cannot imagine at this moment how far I will be from them all in six months.

In Rosa's poem, she remembers the loop her mother allowed her to ride and the first time the men in the factory called out to her, a first catcall from strangers, and her mother's silence when the speaker asks, "Does this mean I am beautiful?" The poem centers on a "pinprick" of a memory, shade and light and then also a metalayer about how memory works, how little we get of it, that pinprick of light, like the shutter of a camera. There's real danger in the speaker's childhood, Drac the Dropout, who bites girls' necks, the boys on the playground who grab asses and teachers who look away, and then the grown men who catcall a girl on a bike with a banana seat. The speaker considers her own daughter's journey on her bike, on safe, quiet streets, and she waits for her too.

I think of the loops in my life, how I never liked to ride the loop in Prospect Park. I prefer to wander on my bike, take whatever turn feels right. Pandemic time is loop time. Slack return and recurrence of very little. Tiny Tim with his little crutch hobbling along, trying to stay alive.

*WEEK THREE*
*MAY 17, 2020*

# LEX AD WITH HAIL

I knew Gina would say no. She almost always says no. As if no is the only option, and maybe it is. What can I expect from casual? What can I ask for?

It's not like I didn't plan ahead. Before the lockdown I made two possible bubbles for myself—one with Gina, one with Guapo and his girlfriend. I take my solitude hard, like I'm at a middle school dance and left alone against the padded gym wall, unworthy—not quarantine material.

Gina and I text-fight.

"It's fine she said no, but I don't even get to be part of the conversation. Your ex has all the power and I have none. You have a straight relationship and still think straight."

"We're not ready. I told you my family comes first."

"You always say that like I don't know, like I'm an idiot, like I'm not a parent too."

She ignores me for big chunks of time. My texts hang in the ether. Perhaps I'm being unreasonable.

I push, she digs in. It feels hopeless.

I type, type, type this chapter. My dean says they will buy me dictation software. Last year I tried to register my disability with the Office of Equal Opportunity. I am told there is no mechanism for employees to register, but I can ask for the things I need. Last year I asked for my classes to be closer together on campus because it's hard for me to walk longer distances in short periods of time. Instead the Office offered me a wheelchair. I was so angry I wrote something nasty back and deleted the whole thread. I should have accepted the wheelchair so I could have given it to someone who needed it.

This time, they say I can have the dictation software. I have to buy it myself, but I'll be reimbursed. It's a victory.

There's a second message on Lex from the Germ Bubbler. I take a look. He's a very cute trans man named Beemer. He writes, "What did you figure out about pods and risk and such? My pod is my kid's mother and her bf. It's an okay situation but not great for the long haul."

"I haven't figured out much and I am lonely."

We get off Lex and text and text. I want to go toward energy, toward yes, not no. Negotiation, not hierarchy. Queer, not straight ideology. Gina and I have been fighting about availability for most of our relationship. I love her, but like all my relationships since I came out, something is off. What I want, she cannot give me: Partnership. Commitment. A willingness to bend and shift with me.

Beemer asks for a socially distanced walk and rides into Manhattan to see me. He is just as cute in person as in his photos, and he's smart too, older than me, and established.

We are cold on a bench, but the conversation is easy. We show our lips and nose once as a tease, but we are well-behaved, keep our distance and our masks on. Skaters *clack clack clack* nearby.

Later I ride Lana to a faraway, nicer grocery store on A and Houston. I wear mittens it's so cold.

Inside I wander the aisles, marveling at the fresh produce and gluten-free cookies I haven't seen in weeks. There's beef that's not about to expire, and everyone is fully masked. The cashiers are behind two layers of plexiglass. I find shampoo and conditioner, which I've been out of for a couple days. I don't buy much, but it's enough to make me feel better, to feel fed. Raspberries for my kid, a treat now. We haven't had raspberries in almost two months.

When I get outside, it's hailing. Late spring and little white balls hit the pavement. My seat is wet, just like the street. Little flurries around my eyes. I'm afraid to ride in the hail, but I need to get home. It's my first time buying groceries with Lana. I talk to her because who else is there but me and my bike in this hailpocalypse?

"We can do this. This is why we're together."

I fiddle for a long time with the lock, basket, and bag of groceries, trying to arrange everything for optimum balance, and then I push off and into the bike lane. Lana is steady and strong. I go slow and brake gently. I turn onto A and eventually into the bike lane on Third. The sky is pearly white, like the inside of an oyster shell, and I wonder if there will be a rainbow.

On a corner, taped to a streetlamp, I see a sign, wet from melting hail. "Le Monocle," it reads, like the disappearing Lex ad. There are black-and-white photos from the era. Brassaï took these so many years ago. An underground, forbidden world of butches in beautiful suits and tuxes, femmes in elegant dresses and stacked heels. Dancing cheek to cheek, lined up at the bar, staring into the camera. A dare. I pull the sign off the pole, and it rips in my hands. Too wet. My hands are freezing. Whatever writing was at the bottom is no longer legible, washed out by the hail.

I fold it carefully into fours and slide it into the cup of my bra—the safest place for anything really: next to a hot, beating, wanting heart. The paper is cold next to my boob. I pedal on.

We make it home safely. Me and Lana. We don't fall, so we don't have to get up.

I cuddle under a blanket on the couch with my cat, take the paper out of my bra, and spread it out on a couch cushion. The sexy photos of Parisian queer nightlife are smeared into a rainbow. I can make out just one word—"Flatbush"—and write it down in my notebook so I don't forget. I haven't ridden my bike on Flatbush yet, but it's a street I know well.

I remember the Lex promise, *We'll find you*, and I say "Yeah, right" into the empty living room.

At some point Beemer texts me, "You're the pretty one here. The hot one. Also, I like that you're super smart and cute. You're a catch."

I feel so stunned by this text, so much that I don't really know what to text back. So far we've just shared research on germ bubbles, how other countries are doing them, "double bubbling" in Canada, and how we might try to see each other again.

"Lol, I haven't felt like a catch in some time," I text back, then fall asleep.

To feel like a treasure, to be valued, to be called cute and hot, a catch. I haven't really heard any of that language since I came out. Or it hasn't registered as real when I've heard it a couple of times.

The next morning I text back, "I like that you think I'm a catch."

"It's true."

# RUIN PORN

After a day of terrible heartburn, I take Lana out for a ride. I push off from Fourth Street and head east. It's colder than I thought it would be, and my hands start to ache. No matter, I keep pedaling.

It's almost seven p.m. and the streets are empty. The clapping starts when I'm on Delancey, which is mostly businesses, so I don't hear much and I don't stop to clap. Lately I've noticed extra graffiti and tagging, like the city is returning to ruin or to some earlier version of itself that I never saw. New York in the '70s and '80s, ablaze, abandoned by all but the most devoted and those of us with nowhere else to go. As I bike deeper into the Lower East Side and Chinatown, I remember the movie *Downtown 81* that I watched at Metrograph with Guapo last summer. It stars Jean-Michel Basquiat, who plays a wandering graffiti artist, the flaneur of rubble, music, and the lost New York of another favorite movie of mine, *Desperately Seeking Susan.*

My hands freeze and my chest burns with acid. Earlier that day I read about the relationship between IBS and COVID-19. I am trying to pedal away from my body, away from my pain, and maybe I am yet another artist trying to chronicle love among the ruins.

I push past Metrograph and wish I could go in. I want a cocktail and steak tartar, and then I want to watch a movie in the dark with strangers. I'm getting better at stopping and starting and perching on my toes when I stop. I even play a little balancing game when I'm stopped at a light. I lift my feet and dangle them. I don't panic and I'm not afraid.

Later at home, I make a list of the places I don't want to lose. In all my conversations with my artist friends and lovers, we talk about what we're afraid of losing. We worry that this is the final step in the long gentrification of New York City.

- All the art house theaters like Metrograph, Angelika, and Film Forum
- Kiki's cheap Greek food
- The cat café on Rivington where I take my students
- Pieces gay bar
- Henrietta Hudson lesbian bar
- Cubbyhole lesbian bar
- McNally Jackson bookstore
- Codex bookstore
- A café called Little Canal
- All the Chinatown light shops
- The hardware store on Great Jones where I buy my bungee cords
- Whiskers pet shop
- Westville Bakery with its amazing gluten-free carrot cake
- Tile Bar

The grocery store is closed when I arrive, so I keep riding all the way from Avenue A to Hudson, where the other grocery store I love is also closed. It's okay. I am so worried about these workers, I'd rather not buy groceries today.

I text Eurydice and get no response. I'm too mad to text Gina again. I'm planning a dinner with Beemer. The literature on bubbles says it's okay if there are no leaks.

# WEDDING-TENT MORGUE

I'm not *not* writing about death. Most days when I ride, there are ambulances idling on at least five or six streets. I avoid these streets out of respect for the dead or because of my own fear of seeing something I don't want to see.

When I first meet Eurydice, we watch a movie about one of the first lesbian feminist porn makers and then walk through Chinatown. After a while, holding hands, I can't help myself.

"I love you," I say. Maybe it's too soon, but I do.

"I love you too. You're easy to love, why not?" she says, and the "Why not?" gives me a moment's pause, but we're interrupted by sirens.

Flashing lights; a fire truck sprays water into a building totally consumed by flames. The police haven't had time to block off the street and so there are gawkers, the people who can't look away. I'm always afraid of seeing too much, of having an image seared into my memory. I regret most horror movies I've watched because certain images haunt me: Carol Anne gets yanked under the bed by the evil clown doll, her brother is swallowed by a tree, the Indigenous peoples' cemetery deservedly swallows their house whole, a dripping woman with black eyes crawls along a wooden floor, there's something wrong with her neck, your father is a zombie now, destined to chase you through London, into the Tube, into the countryside.

We scurry across the street. The firemen can't control the flames and the street is hot. Because I'm Orpheus, I look back and see a charred body on a gurney and then we run. When we get back to my place, we fuck and then cry as if we can erase what we saw with tearful orgasms.

To live in the city now is to bear witness to bodies, not people so much as corpses. Guapo says one in four hundred New Yorkers have died, and he's right. Every hospital now has a makeshift morgue in the form of a white wedding tent next to it. Refrigerated trucks are full of bodies, and funeral homes can't keep up. Some people know ten people who have died, while I know two.

Am I hunting for the corpse of my first relationship with a woman, whatever that magical time once was that I can't get over? Am I forever looking back and trying to reanimate what we once had?

# QUEERS DISAPPEAR

Disappearing queers.

Can I have some tears for your fears?

Queers equal tears.

The CityMD isn't crowded. There are three people ahead of me. Two young men behind me loudly discuss the futility of online dating now. One has an amazing ass and a red bandanna.

"I have so many matches."

"Right?"

"But I'm like, what's the point?"

Inside I get both the antibody and the COVID-19 tests. They are free. I'm in New York City. I'm lucky. The only thing that stresses me out is the iPad login. I should have wiped it down. The ID scanner is dirty.

I keep my bike helmet and mask on the whole time. The doctor has full PPE, with a mask and shield.

"We have to use a vein in your wrist," she says because my veins suck.

"Sit on your hands while I do the nasal swab." I do. I am always a good patient.

"Three to five days," she says, and puts a Band-Aid on me. "Be safe on your bike!"

## KID INTERLUDE

Mostly I write when I don't have my kid, when she's with her dad, Guapo, and his wonderful girlfriend, Pauline. Pauline and I are close now, but it took a while. It's my fault. I was jealous of their relationship in the beginning and I didn't ask her enough about her life. Now we talk about her dreams and dissertation, tease Guapo about his dad jokes, and make him drive us places for fried chicken, which feels perfect to me. I love her now and she loves my kid and my kid loves her.

You might hear me mention my kid and not write about her and think I'm some kind of mom, but I like to give her space. You know? Only moms get asked why they do or don't write about their kids.

People ask sometimes during this pandemic, mostly nonparents, "How is she? How is she coping?"

I say, "She has an online gaming world that helps her so much. She can finally sleep according to her sleep cycle, but she misses her friends."

I don't talk as much about her anxiety. Her fears for the future. The world we're in, that nobody imagined 2020 would be so bad.

There are sirens every night. First for death, and then for protests for cops murdering Black people.

I can tell you that the online world of Roblox, where my kid and her friends meet up, is both magical and mundane. Sometimes when I look over her shoulder, her avatar is wearing a Pride jumpsuit and a bouffant purple wig while flying around with giant black eagle wings that span a building that she herself has built. Other times, she's just a pixelated, bigger-thighed version of herself delivering pizza on a scooter to make more money for the game. Read Roland Barthes's essay "Toys" now if you feel like it and do some freewriting about a toy that prepared you for capitalism and a toy that taught you to resist it.

I can also tell you that, like so many of the kids I know and teach today, she's a sweet radical. When she finds out I've been out protesting against the murder of George Floyd and for Black Lives Matter, she sends me a TikTok for how to treat myself and anyone else if we get tear-gassed.

"I'm being careful," I text back.

"Everyone needs to know." And she's right.

*WEEK FOUR*
*MAY 24, 2020*

# HE'S CALLED BEEMER BECAUSE

He picks me up in a BMW. Later he will correct me on the brand of his car. Beemer and I have agreed to make a bubble and have checked with our exes that it's okay with them to expand our bubbles. We agree no pressure for a relationship, just two older queers who need touch and companionship.

His house is really nice—a renovated brownstone with built-ins. Two floors belong to him and his eight-year-old daughter, and the top two belong to his ex. He makes me dinner and a negroni. We go for a walk and talk a lot about academia, probably too much, because I am so lonely and desperate for touch I am not listening to the panic inside me, or I don't hear it.

Or I am so desperate for care that I don't recognize how I really feel, that maybe something is off, that this is all moving very quickly.

"Should we just kiss to get it over with so I can calm down?" I ask, thinking this is funny and also true.

He says, "I'm a slow burn," so I think that means no, and I feel my usual shame attack for asking for something and not getting it.

Still, I'm game. I tell myself not to panic. We'd decided earlier over text that we wouldn't have sex, just talk and cuddle. So we talk on the couch about my books, about his kid's toys, many of which are the same as my kid's and set up in little configurations around the living room.

"Do you want to lie on the bed?" he asks, and I say yes.

We're both good kissers, that part is a match, and some of my clothes are coming off. My shirt and my bra. His shirt. My pants.

"I want to check in because I thought you didn't want to have sex," I say.

"I think I changed my mind," he says.

"Are you sure?"

"Yeah."

And then he's licking my pussy and he's very good at that and then I am licking his pussy, and I've really missed pussies.

He says he wants me to stay overnight and I don't think I want to, but I do anyway, because he will have to drive me home and that makes me feel bad. I'm also afraid to ride back from Brooklyn alone on my bike in the middle of the night over the Manhattan Bridge, which I've never been on, and know to be narrow and dark.

I don't sleep very well, and I feel him awake in the night, anxious. I like him a lot, but I am also thinking about Gina, whom I'd rather be next to but can't because she won't or can't make a germ bubble with me.

In the morning he is awkward, and I don't understand. He insists on making me breakfast, and I get stressed because something has shifted and I don't know why or what. It feels like the aftermath of a bad college hookup—like, get out, you have to go, but stay, no, really, I like you, you're special. He's nervous about his daughter coming down the stairs and seeing me.

"It's a bit intense for me," I say. "I haven't dated anyone whose kid lives just upstairs."

"It's not ideal for dating."

I'm ready to go. His dog chews on my bike helmet while we eat, but I wear it anyway and leave with my uneasy feelings.

The ride home is long and I make a wrong turn and for one terrifying minute I am almost on the BQE. I wheel my bike through some weeds and then back onto the highway to access the bike path. I think of Dionne and Cher in *Clueless* and the hilarious scene when they get on the Los Angeles freeway and scream for a full minute until they can exit. I wish I had someone to scream and laugh with me, to witness my accidents and mistakes. Being a ham and making people laugh is one of my great joys. I don't get to do that much anymore, except for with my kid.

On the Manhattan Bridge, the sky opens up and rains on me. The bridge is slick so I go extra slow. It's narrow, like I feared. People pass me, and I get rattled. Sometimes I have a little spasm and do a jerky handlebar thing.

A woman cruises by and shouts, "Are you okay?"

"Yes!" I say back.

The rain stops and I'm off the bridge. The city is quiet. It's only eight a.m. When I get to the corner of Houston and Allen, I pull up next to a middle-aged white guy in a beat-up, dusty-rose convertible Cadillac. He beams at me. No mask.

"Nice car," I say.

"Thanks, my wife says I shouldn't be out here. I have asthma, but there's no pollution! The air is so clean!"

I look away and wait for the light to change so I can escape. He seems a little unhinged, and I don't want him to breathe on me.

He points to a rooftop kitty-corner to where we wait. "Did you ever see that lighthouse up there?"

I look up and he's right. There's a cute little painted lighthouse, almost like a treehouse fort, on top of the building.

"No, I haven't seen that!" I'm delighted with him now.

"Wouldn't it be fun to live up there?" he says, and before I can reply, the light changes and he speeds off.

## I FALL AND I CAN'T GET UP

This last winter, long before I got Lana, I fall on the street so spectacularly that I break my arm. My mom is in town, and we fight in the vicious ways of my family. Duress I am not allowing myself to write about.

Am I mentally ill? Yes. I have breakdowns. Episodes. Bodily manifestations of psychological trauma. Also perimenopause is for real and there's very little research on how to help perimenopausal women—because, guess what, nobody cares.

My kid and I rush down University Place. I haven't slept well and, as my therapist will later point out, my boundaries have been obliterated. One wrong step and my foot catches on a seam in the sidewalk, or maybe some mottled part or maybe nothing, and then I'm down, collapsed, Lana Turner has collapsed. I hear a bone break, a rattle, a fissure, slippage, wrongness.

"Mama, are you okay?"

"No, no. I think my arm is broken," I say, helpless. Remember when we could touch each other, when strangers could help you on the street?

"Mama," my kid says.

A construction worker pulls me up with my good arm. Street murmurs and a woman behind me cooing softly. I cradle my arm and realize I need to console my kid, reassure her that I'm all right.

"You run ahead. Meet your friend. Mama will go to the doctor. I'm okay, don't worry." I watch her go.

I do a bizarre amount of chores for someone with a broken arm, get my medicine, pack a bag, call Guapo and Pauline to find out the best emergency room to go to, get in a cab, and feel lucky for the millionth time that I have insurance.

At the hospital, I beg for Percocet and weep. I am always afraid of getting stuck somewhere without my medicine. The nurses are so nice. I get a second Percocet.

# HACKS

It's hard to fix the mistakes that the robot makes while I talk. Going back in and editing hurts my muscles too. I am trying to hack the novel. This serialization, this robot, this way of writing this book—it's all a trick to make something I find excruciating easier. Writing my last novel gave me a nervous breakdown.

I see most of my friends working, working, working, working; Zooming to keep businesses going, clients happy, bosses satisfied; the capitalist machine running, running, running. Humming. I am typing now because I don't feel like fixing all the mistakes on the robot dictator. This software really isn't that great. Just so you know, I couldn't get Dragon so am using Microsoft Word. I shouldn't complain, but I'm a complainer, so I will do that here.

I start reading *Heavy* by Kiese Laymon, and it's already the best thing ever and there's something in the beginning about not giving the reader what she wants or not giving the publisher the lie that they want or not giving the audience the triumphant narrative. What it means, though, is that I have to expose myself in all my wretchedness, or it feels that way.

If I were to describe depression to you, I mean, could I? Could I describe mental illness with a side of neurological disorder? Or maybe it's the other way around. No one's brain is going to be right when there's not enough dopamine and when the serotonin doesn't jump the synapses the way it's supposed to. I'm a very smart woman, but even when my neurologist draws me pictures of my brain, it makes no sense to me. It's quite baffling to her at times too, and she's an expert in movement disorders.

I have the wrong code to get reimbursed for therapy. Or I have left off a number and now I have to resubmit the claims.

Depression, for me, is not being able to stop crying for a whole day. It's acute sensitivity, a blowing up of slights others might consider minor. It's fighting when you don't want to, it's escalating when you should stand down, it's not seeing anything up ahead that looks good or fun or interesting or hopeful, it's no end in sight, it's a pandemic for sure—but what's mental illness housed inside of a pandemic? Suicide, I fear.

For all my life, I have received or helped shape or believed a message that I am not lovable or worthy of the kinds of love I need. It's humiliating to type this. It makes me cry even more and I am currently very medicated. So medicated that I am thirty pounds overweight even though I have no appetite.

My friend Picasso messages me on Insta that I'm too hung up on coming out late. "There's no such thing as a good queer. Being queer is failure."

"Yes, I've read my Halberstam," I write back.

"Don't try to be such a good girl and a good queer," he writes, and I feel momentarily liberated from myself, which is nice when you are mentally ill.

# MEMORIAL DAY

On Memorial Day, I take Lana for a long ride. We navigate a giant square, up First Avenue to Fifty-Second Street, all the way west down Eleventh Avenue, and back into the Village. The city is especially empty except for, as always, the delivery people, the grocery store workers, and the doctors, nurses, and hospital staff. On First Avenue I pass Bellevue, pause, and take a picture of a place I might have wound up in if it weren't for my doctors and medication.

A sweet Black man smiles at me and says, "You're taking my picture, right? Because I'm so handsome."

I laugh through my mask and say, "I am. Yes, you are."

I ride past the hospital and see people in scrubs. They look tired of course. One woman leans into the open window of a car. I imagine this is her husband she is visiting and I pedal on.

The UN building is amazing! Why don't I know this already? Lana is teaching me the architecture of New York City, about buildings I've ignored or have never really looked at.

I cross Fifty-Second Street slowly. There's a middle-aged white woman on a foldable bike. She and I alternate passing each other—it's not competitive, just that we both take our time. There's something beautiful in our continual, gentle passing of each other. I've needed more cyclists like her, who are less focused on the speed and more about the ride itself. We loop each other, a dance in an empty city. I vow when the pandemic is over to start a Slow Riders Club. In my fantasy version of this club we take over the street and go incredibly slow, a wrench in the path of speedy cyclists and capitalism.

Lana, cover your ears—but for my next bike, I'd like a foldable one. My bike guy says they are wonderful, well-designed, and worth the extra money.

On Fifty-Second and Park or Madison I see a long food line, mostly men and a few women waiting to be fed. I slow down for the light and make sure to take them into my brain and heart. How hard it is to be hungry and wait in line for food. Don't glide easily or bumpily past. See who is there and what they need.

When I get to Forty-Second Street, Times Square, it's empty except for me, a photographer with a tripod set up, and the Jesus-sign guy, who has arranged all of his signs around the Winter Garden theater:

"Jesus is the way."

"Jesus loves you."

"Christ died for our sins."

"Whosoever shall call upon the Lord shall be saved."

"Jesus sayeth, I am the way, the truth, and the life."

"By grace are you saved through faith, not of works."

I sweat and pant into my mask. I want to take this emptiness in and hold it still. The Jesus guy, is this his panpocalypse, the rapture?

I keep heading west past an old apartment in Hell's Kitchen and down Eleventh Avenue. The Javits Center appears on my right, and then the gleaming, silver subway cars idling in the sun, like loaves of bread waiting to rise.

I pedal down and over into Chelsea. I stare through the window of a bookstore. I miss book browsing, touching the beautiful objects that I read and write.

In Chelsea I start to smell hot dogs and it's only then that I feel sad. I love a hot dog with mustard on a grill. The only things I really like about holidays are the food and my people. I haven't eaten enough.

Near Stonewall, which is closed, a bar is doing curbside service. I order a negroni and french fries, and I wheel my bike to the park across from Stonewall. I sit six feet from the other loners. My negroni seems to be 100 percent gin. I haven't had a drink this strong in three months. Gin makes me stupid and angry. I only have three sips and then scroll through Eurydice's Twitter and Instagram. She looks good, skinnier than when I last saw her, but totally fine, like she's handling lockdown with the swagger of someone who doesn't need anyone, who is keeping it all together. What do I know? I text her something stupid about hot dogs and being friends again maybe.

No response.

I ride home and eat something. My joy returns to me—I had such a long and beautiful ride. I feel certain and balanced on Lana, this is a big shift for me, for us. I get into bed, reread parts of *Inferno* by Eileen Myles, and think about jokes—how jokes were the protagonist's first good thing, a way to make the mothers sitting on the stoop in her neighborhood laugh. I'm also rereading *Later* by Paul Lisicky and admiring him for his honest sadness around sex and love. Please imagine these books as inspiration for this book. This semester I teach adrienne maree brown's *Emergent Strategy*.

Is this writing an attempt to craft some emergent strategy, a fractal approach to art-making in the face of totalitarianism, plague, the carceral state, and white supremacy's capitalist death cult? I dedicate this book to adrienne maree brown, Paul Lisicky, and Eileen Myles. I dedicate it to the protesters, George Floyd and his family, Breonna Taylor, Tony McDade, Nina Pop, Monika Diamond, Sandra Bland, and everyone who has died from police brutality, murder, and COVID-19.

Please remember that joy is an act of resistance. I used to make people laugh, when I could see them. I miss making you laugh. I will try harder for joy.

# BLACK LIVES MATTER

Riding back from Brooklyn, I intersect with protesters and join them. Several of us are on bikes, and people carry signs that read "Black Lives Matter" and "Justice for George Floyd." We all know what's happening because there's no justice for Black and Brown people in America. I teach a course called Youth in Revolt and have no illusions about the police because I know the history of social movements in this country and abroad. What's happening now is connected to COINTELPRO and the state-sanctioned murder of Fred Hampton and the attempted framing of Angela Davis. The list goes on. If you've been paying attention at all, you know what the police do.

The cops run alongside us until we get to Houston, and then police vans pull up and try to get us out of the street. We are all masked and most of the protesters are young. They run and ride quickly. I have been learning to slow down and speed up.

We chant:

"Fuck the police!"

"No justice, no peace!"

"George Floyd!"

"Breonna Taylor!"

There are maybe two hundred protesters, and the cops keep running next to us, trying to cut us off with scooters, and swarming to arrest people who step into the street. It's easy for me to use my white body as a buffer. The police ignore me, and aside from chanting I am silent behind my mask.

We make it to Zuccotti Park. Two more arrests, cops swarming with their plastic handcuffs. I protest a lot, but I've never been arrested because I am afraid I won't be given my medicine in jail and also because of my childhood. I am afraid of violence. These are choices I've made, though I recognize my comfort and privilege.

At Zuccotti Park I feel a surge of pride. A couple of protesters shout "Occupy Wall Street!" and I'm taken back to that radical time, and to my first novel, a protest novel. But we keep moving.

I'm slow and some of us get disconnected from the larger group. I forget about the pandemic because this is more important. I pedal hard to catch up. At the base of the Freedom Tower there are hundreds of cops chasing the protesters. The irony doesn't elude me.

I speed ahead and join up again at Battery Park City. More clashing. Swatting. A cop rips a bicycle away from a Black woman who fights to get it back. She does and we cheer. More dispersal and jogging. I rest with my bike. I notice a little subgroup of queer teens and feel tender toward them.

Eventually I cycle onto the West Side Highway to meet up with the protesters again. There are more of us on bikes now, and the cyclists stay in the street both behind and ahead of the protesters while sirens flash, cops run, and scooters keep trying to intersect us. They arrest a Latinx teenage girl who starts crying, and we record her and say, "Shout your name! Shout your name so we can find you!" and she does.

Another group of young protesters link arms across the highway and try to block a wall of cops who keep repeating their drone robot bullhorn recording: "If you don't get out of the street, we're going to arrest you. If you don't get out of the street, we're going to arrest you. You are blocking traffic. You are blocking traffic."

Some of these protesters are not much older than my kid. The cops try to surround them, but the bikes, our bikes, are in the way. Filming. Filming.

It's a chase. It's been a long chase and my knees are burning.

The protesters get smart and throw garbage bags into the street to block the scooters and vans. We maneuver our bikes around the garbage onto Chambers Street and then onto Church. A white man yells at us about the garbage, and the protesters tell him to fuck off and care about the right things.

For a couple glorious minutes, it's just twenty people on bikes hooting with joy. The only women I see are myself and the woman who fought to get her bike back. I feel a kind of rare boy butch anonymity. A white twentysomething manboy asks me, "Yo, how do I get to the Williamsburg Bridge?" and I tell him.

The police-scooter swarm catches up and cuts us off. I almost fall off my bike. I cut my ankle but keep pedaling and manage to get around the cops. Up ahead is another trap. My hands start shaking and I feel like I might fall again if I keep riding, so I leave.

When I get home I post all my videos and describe what I saw. My colleague asks if she can have the footage for her website, Ark Republic, a radical Black creative media outlet. Absolutely. I'm on social media for a long time after that. It keeps me up and makes my solitude more palpable to me. Tonight felt extra brutal. Cops chasing kids of color for hours.

The last image I see tonight is a Minneapolis police precinct on fire. From my posts, a couple of friends check in. How to tell them that I was not afraid because I was fine. I'm white. I am fine, mostly. It's just that I started to get tremors and tics so I had to go home.

Do you know what a tic is or a tremor? Do you know how many people of color suffer from chronic health problems like fibromyalgia, lupus, asthma, and diabetes? They are no strangers to muscle pain. The whole country is in massive pain, both medicated and unmedicated. Collectively we are traumatized by the legacies of genocide and slavery, and since so many white people are in denial about this trauma, the grief and pain of it, we have an increasingly unwell country.

I protest for two more days until I hurt my knees and can't walk for a day.

What I love most about neurology is the connection between the "it" and the "I," the body and the soul, the brain and the psyche, which is also what people call the body politic.

*WEEK FIVE*
*MAY 31, 2020*

# WISE SLUTITUDE

#BlackLivesMatter
#PublishingPaidMe
#JKRowlingIsaTERF
#FuckthePolice
#NYCProtests

Put the world in the book. The book is the world.

I don't go outside for a couple days. I'm taking care of my kid, but I get lost on Twitter. Scrolling, scrolling, posting, obsessively checking hashtags.

My kid goes to visit my mom upstate for two weeks, and so now for these next forty or so pages, I will be like parents in TV shows and movies—a mom who doesn't seem like a mom, or who has silent, largely off-screen interactions with boring kids who kinda roll with it. I love the brutal bickering codependence of the white married people on that show *Catastrophe*, but it's wild to me how quiet and docile their toddler and baby are. Little props that are gloriously fitting for the couple's narcissism.

What's going on in the #CapitolHillAutonomousZone? Of course I need to know. I wrote a book set during Occupy Wall Street. I live for takeovers of public space. Twitter reveals very little except for a lot of alt-right Nazis claiming that this is a terrorist act by antifa. I give up, my brain scrambled from spending too much time alone scrolling on social media.

While Guapo drives our kid upstate, I spend a lovely afternoon napping and pooping. My stomach is always a mess. I have IBS and am taking some prescription thing for heartburn. It's nice and rare for me to get everything out. A cleansing.

When I wake up I have a message on Lex from the disappearing ad. It reads, "If you want to go to Le Monocle and touch a queer, you'll have to pass. Do not share this link with anyone."

The link takes me to a Google Form. I fill it out:

> **List the people you have touched in the last two months.**
> *My kid, my ex-husband, his girlfriend, and one date who I saw once for sex.*
>
> **What lockdown protocols have you taken in the last two months to protect yourself?**
> *Aside from seeing the above four people, I have quarantined myself in my apartment except to go on bike rides, to get groceries, and to get a COVID test. Whenever I leave the apartment, I wear a mask and practice social distancing. I wash my hands vigorously many times a day.*
>
> **What is your antibody status?**
> *Negative for antibodies. Negative for COVID.*
>
> **What talents do you bring to the club?**

(My fingers hover over the keyboard. What to say? Is this a trick question? What talents have I brought to any club ever, not least a secret underground queer club operating during a pandemic?)

> *Wise slutitude and excellent communication skills.*

I hit Submit and shut my computer. I've hated gay bars ever since I came out, I remind myself. The flirting rituals are wholly confusing and mostly I feel unwanted and old in queer spaces.

The Google Form is a known boner killer.

"Fuck it," I say out loud to the no one, the nobody, the no-people-ness of my apartment.

# PAIN

Like the sockets joining my pelvis to my legs are aflame. Like my knee bones need an appointment with the muscles around them. "There's anger and hurt in our hips," a yoga teacher said once long ago, in the time of classes and community, and I burst into tears.

In the bathtub I press on a constellation of new bruises along my inner knees and shins. Painless compared to the rest. Deep down in the muscle and tissue of my neck and right shoulder there is a baby I used to hold on that same side for one whole year. I favor my right side in all things, because when I can't walk, when I am very sick, the left side is always worse. I don't have cerebral palsy, though it is one of my misdiagnoses. People with CP understand the drag and pull of an unresponsive part of your body. In the "before" time, when I was very sick, I dragged my left leg behind me like a ghost or a small corpse. My left hand and arm curled in so tightly that they sometimes cramped, like the letter *C*, but in pain.

# DON'T WRITE ABOUT ME

I check in on Beemer, my supposed pandemic lover.

"You want a relationship and that's not where I'm at right now," he texts.

"I thought we just agreed on companionship, a germ bubble, maybe sex."

"You're right, I'm projecting. I don't have a lot of experience with sex outside of a relationship."

"Why did we have sex then?" I text back. "We didn't need to have sex."

"I think it's best if we don't have contact."

"Why? What happened?"

I am so confused. What have I done? I go to the bad places—my body, my desires, somehow. In one night, I managed to convey too much need. Teenage shame thoughts too. I'm fat. He doesn't like the taste of my pussy.

I cry my queer tears. I cry my slut tears. I feel betrayed and accused of things I have not done.

"And please don't write about me," he texts.

"I can do what I want." I am defiant, then ashamed. Is that what this is about? My being a writer? I feel bullied and block him.

Maybe this is a metaphor for academia. Contract and adjunct faculty cannot fuck tenured faculty. Autofiction has always been located in the femme space of the contract and the adjunct. I know I'm lucky to have a contract, but I do not own a brownstone with my ex who is also tenured, and I can't recognize a BMW to save my life. But my writing life is my own, and because I am small, indie, and nontenured, I have been able to keep it mostly on my own terms. For me this is more important than money, though I could use some more of that too.

# DON'T LOOK BACK

Instagram says I have a memory and tells me that two years ago today I was on a trip with Eurydice. My face is a different face, thinner, younger, framed by a tight, nice haircut—not my pandemic face, which is haggard, bored, framed by a gray mullet. I can't believe it was only two years ago. Maybe that's why I'm not over her. The pandemic, the Trump presidency, everything that's happened this year, my medicine—they have all disrupted my notions of time. Will I ever be over her? Can I stop looking back over my shoulder at the woman who shoved me out of the closet? Who didn't care that I had a boyfriend? Who refused to make space for him even though we were in an open relationship? The woman who left her wife, then decided not to be with me.

The photo is a selfie. I'm in my bathing suit against an adobe wall smirking, because I had just come out and fallen in love with the most amazing woman I'd ever met. Eurydice. I am not dealing with the loss of my boyfriend, whom I love very much still. He broke into my apartment drunk and scared us one night, and I cannot forgive him for that.

Seeing the photo brings back the memory of that whole trip. I had gotten a new credit card and taken us to Santa Fe that June, which is like going to Hades it's so hot. But Georgia O'Keefe went there and it's a town full of lesbians and I have a friend there and Eurydice wants to go to Meow Wolf. My kid has been there with her dad and she wants me to go too.

"Mama, there's a refrigerator that's a tunnel into another room and a bone dinosaur you can play like a keyboard."

Our first day there, Eurydice and I fuck the fucks of falling in love, and because I am mentally ill, I'm slightly manic, maybe very manic. I haven't put a trip on a credit card since college, when I signed up for a Discover card because they were giving away giant Krackel bars. Who doesn't want a giant Krackel bar? Fifteen years and fifteen thousand dollars later, I will still stand by that candy bar.

I spend the afternoon in the hotel pool while Eurydice naps. She's always tired because she works so much. I walk up and down the length of the kidney-shaped pool, get out, apply sunscreen, try to read my book and fail, and get back in the water. Over and over again.

When a family comes into the pool area—mother, father, toddler, and baby—I talk to them in ways I don't talk to people in New York.

"What brings you to Santa Fe?" I ask. My shoulders are burning, I can tell. There's no amount of sunscreen that can block this desert sun. Even the pool water is warm.

"Business for him." The mom nods at the dad, who is indistinct to me. A man. I don't know. I am mad at men because of what my boyfriend did. "We're just tagging along."

The toddler has water wings on and splashes from the pool steps. The mom floats the baby around and makes bubbles with her the way all moms do. The endless building of language acquisition that moms are never acknowledged for, which basically creates civilization.

"Oh yes, you're in the water now. Doesn't that feel nice? Blow a bubble. Splash. Splash," she says to the happy baby. "What about you?" she asks me.

"I'm here with my girlfriend, just a romantic getaway," I say, and they roll with it, are not homophobic, at least at that moment. It is such a thrill for me to say, *I'm here with my girlfriend. My girlfriend.* I've never had a girlfriend. I've made out with women for years and have had endless crushes that I thought were just intense friendships, or maybe this is how it is for bi/pan people. We figure stuff out when we do. Whatever.

Eurydice opens our room window, which faces the pool. "Babe," she calls down to me, and for a second I think I'm in trouble. To be in trouble with her is not fun, and so I avoid conflict, mostly in the form of not asking for too much, letting her take the lead. She can be a total bitch when she's angry, and I'm not used to women being angry with me like that.

But she's smiling. Sleepy, but not grouchy. "Come up? Let's go get food?"

I shrug at the couple like, *You know, girlfriends, so hungry! Gotta keep them happy!*

I get out of the pool, a little self-conscious about my feet, which are the only visibly disabled part of me. But fuck it, Eurydice loves me. Who cares?

Up in the hotel room, there is so much licking and then we go out for Mexican food. An old-school place where we meet my friend, also a lesbian, whom I have known since graduate school and love very much. Eurydice is competitive with her about weird things and my friend doesn't take the bait. I feel embarrassed, but I drown the feeling in margaritas and bean enchiladas slathered in cheese and sour cream.

When we were in New York, in her tiny Washington Heights apartment, which sits atop three different hills, Eurydice cooked for me. Many different delicious kinds of eggs mostly and sometimes dishes pulled together from the cupboard. One time, we tackled a Blue Apron box that someone gave her. We loved the little packets of ingredients. Things I'm personally too lazy to buy or never have the energy to care about. We cooked in our underwear and marveled at what we had become.

I don't ever want to lose that, so in Santa Fe I pretend nothing is wrong, and that in the fall she will still be my girlfriend.

# META

My robot dictator isn't working again, so I'm typing. It's faster anyway, and I have a deadline, which is my own fault. I pitched this project to Feminist Press as a partially serialized novel. It was my idea to set a constraint for myself so I wouldn't be able to stop writing. In the last year, I've started and stopped five different novels, anywhere from five to a hundred pages long. I sent each one to my agent, and each time she told me to keep going. Eventually she dropped me, which was devastating, but something that happens all the time. Agents are allowed to drop their clients. She wrote simply, "I don't know how to help you anymore," which is baffling, and sounds a lot like something my mom would say when we'd fight.

As long as I don't type for too long, I tell myself, my shoulder won't be in too much pain. Microsoft Word keeps jamming and doing the you're-fucked rainbow swirl, and then I lose the writing I've just dictated. What do you do when the hack doesn't work right? What if you get leg braces and they make it worse and actually deform your feet and make life miserable for a year? That happened to me. Disabled people get experimented on all the time. Touched and groped against their will. Made to try out dumb things and then not listened to about their pain.

My friend Richard Scott Larson wrote an essay that helps me understand what I'm doing in whatever writing life I've managed to cobble together. In "On the Origins of Queer Autofiction: A Review of Dorothy Strachey's 'Olivia,'" Larson writes:

> Queer writers have long taken to the use of autofiction as a dominant storytelling mode. . . . Autofiction—fiction drawn from life, sometimes in almost photorealistic detail—allows for both obfuscation and exaggeration, but it also creates a kind of necessary distance, a

way for a writer to give shape and structure to often painful lived experiences, and thus to reclaim control over them.

*Photorealistic detail*
*Obfuscation and exaggeration*
*Painful experiences*
*Reclaim control over them*

Yes, exactly this, yes.

# ANTIBODIES

My friend Picasso asks me to meet up for a walk. Once, when we first met, we had sex, or we tried to have sex but were interrupted by his roommate's stupid knocking right as I was about to make him come all over my face. He was so rattled he sent me home, and since then, Friendsville.

I haven't seen him since lockdown started.

"Are we hugging?" I ask.

"Yes," he says, and it feels good to touch and smell him.

We walk west to Stonewall then to Cubbyhole. I am getting a blister but I don't say anything. We sit in a pocket park with the other masked queers.

"How are you?" he asks.

"Remember the Beemer guy I texted you about? I think that was a bad experience. I feel tricked, but maybe he just didn't like me." My mask absorbs my tears. "Are you allowed to have sex? Am I allowed to have sex?"

"Nobody knows," he says. "I mean, we know, but it's not sustainable for depressed, single queer people to never touch."

"I'm negative for COVID," I blurt, and then regret it. We are a couple blocks from what used to be St. Vincent's Hospital, and I feel historical/ahistorical. I never wanted to be one of those queers who cares about disease status, blood work, antibodies.

"That's a relief," he says. "I need to ease my mind too and get the test."

"It was easy. But I don't have the antibodies. I don't know anyone who does yet."

"Let's hug more," he says.

I scratch his back like I know he likes. I will take any touch I can get right now. I am touch-starved, a tactile person, a watery Cancer with a Scorpio moon, which I think means I crave stability but cause myself a lot of upheaval.

"Oh, that feels so good," he says, and then he leaves for the train. I want to follow him to Brooklyn. I keep riding my bike there, everyone I care about lives there. I was never meant to be in Manhattan. I have a faculty apartment in a dorm, and in exchange for that apartment, I am a glorified dorm mother. I host dinners, teas, and take students to plays and movies. I reassure parents, and have been very kind and sweet to hundreds of people every year. Sometimes students come to my door at night and tell me they want to die, and I stay with them until we can get help.

It has been been exhausting and lovely, I think as I limp home with my throbbing blistered foot. The dorm is empty—the students left when the pandemic began, though many of their belongings are still in their rooms. I feel like a ghost lady, haunting the halls. The solitude of the building gets unbearable.

Back on the couch, I decide I will move back to Brooklyn. It's been eight years here. I'm going to get kicked out in a year anyway. Why not go before they throw me out?

*WEEK SIX*
*JUNE 7, 2020*

# TOMBOYGIRL

I have long let women and girls tell me what to do. My first crush-slash-best-friend I call Tomboygirl. She's two years older than me and lives around the corner in a house with a piano and beautiful rugs. Her mother listens to calming talk radio that I won't know until college is NPR, and she has two older brothers whom I also worship. Both brothers have long, feathered, blond hair and they both know how to fight. We consider one brother good and one evil, but it's the evil brother who carries me home bleeding one day after I step on a bottle cap. It's romantic, because he looks the most like Tomboygirl, and the neighborhood kids trail behind saying, "Ooooh" and "Ahhh" and "Sitting in a tree, k-i-s-s-i-n-g." He carries me like a bride and I hold on to his neck while trailing blood from my foot. If you think my life is like a fairy tale but just the bloody parts, you are not wrong.

Sometimes when we're bored, Tomboygirl and I press our backs to the evil brother's locked bedroom door and listen to whatever he's listening to, mostly a song about Jojo, a man who thought he was a woman. I am that accident kid, the one who needs protectors. I wasn't supposed to take my shoes off, but the other kids did and the grass felt so nice until the terrible pinch of the rusty bottle cap.

Shoe interlude. Shoe stanza. Shoe paragraph. Robot dictator does not want to learn the word *shoe*.

Tomboygirl has shoes I covet, and because there is something wrong with me that nobody is able to name, I cannot walk in them. Because I cannot accept my deformities, I beg my parents for these shoes. Clogs.

Hers are red with stitching on the top. Her feet are beautiful unlike mine, which are twisted and flat. She slides them on while I wait outside the screen door. Her mother imposes rules that my mother doesn't. I am often not allowed in. Tomboygirl asks permission for everything and yet she is wild and free. The door opens, she runs out, clacking ahead of me, ass tight, long legs, thighs strong in short shorts. I don't understand how the clogs stay on her feet but they do, and I run after her.

Dr. Scholl's sandals. The ads say they massage your feet. My mother thinks they are ridiculous. Tomboygirl runs in these too, but mostly she and two older girls who hate me clack up and down the street talking about grown-up things.

"Things *you* don't understand," Anita of the long, tan legs says to me. I think if I had the Dr. Scholl's I could do this too.

"You'll kill yourself in those," my mother says.

One summer evening at Hills, which is like Kmart but shittier, I see knockoff Dr. Scholl's. To me Hills is still a magical place full of makeup, shoes, records, and jewelry.

I beg and nag. I am known in my family for nagging, for being relentless.

"Please Mommy please Mommy please please please can I have the sandals?"

"Fine, put them in the cart and stop nagging."

When we get home it's twilight. I cut the tags and slip on my fake Dr. Scholl's like Cinderella with her glass slipper. I'm more like a stepsister though, because they hurt. I go outside and find some kids, maybe Cammie, who is younger than me and always around. I clack up and down our block talking about the sandals and how amazing they feel until I get blisters and go home.

"They're just as good as Dr. Scholl's," I say, and I truly think they are beautiful. I love the sound they make against the sidewalk even though they hurt and I think I'm gonna fall. The younger girls nod and take it in. Tomboygirl is not there but I'll show her tomorrow.

I'm mimicking the way my mom and her best friend talk about clothes and shoes: a kind of whimsical necessity, a kind of freedom from their lives as secretaries. I love shopping with my mom; to this day we still have fun doing it.

Later that summer I find scuffed white clogs at a garage sale. I use allowance money to buy them. They have a strap that you can fold back or on top.

These will work, I think to myself—but they hurt just as much. What I love about them in the end is the shoe-polish brush I use to paint them bright white every day. I always sit next to my father while he shines his shoes, but now I have my own pair to fuss over and buff. A butch act. I don't know, I don't understand gender; you tell me.

# HEAD DESTROYER 9000

I get into a thing with my eye. If I wake up tomorrow as a giant bug, don't be surprised. Except for I won't have to worry about coming out of my room and embarrassing my family, because no one is here. I can just be that bug. Lie on the couch like I've done way too much the last three days, on my back, kicking up my disgusting little bug feet and waving my antennae in the air. Beetle on her back. Couch bug. Sad cockroach.

First I think I slept on my face and that's why my eye hurts. Last night I dreamed that my old boyfriend was holding me down and I woke up panicky and grouchy. He never did that in real life, but he was often trying to keep me from doing queer, poly things. Still, I miss him. When I used to get off the couch, he would gently push my butt up to help me stand. It was sweet.

Sore eye. I tell Twitter I slept on my face and only the poet Jim Behrle likes it. He gets it. He understands sleeping on your face.

At night I look more closely in the mirror and see that I'm getting a stye. Googling too much leads me to the beautiful word *chalazion*, plural *chalazia*, which is another kind of eyelid bump caused by contacts or bacteria or a blocked tear duct. I haven't been crying enough. Too stunned to cry. Too medicated to cry. Or I cry in one horrible gush into my mask.

If I am ever to become a Greek goddess, please name me Chalazion—seer and guardian of disabled queers, old women who protest, and sick eyeballs.

My stye distracts me from my couch wallowing. I make hot compresses and take selfies with them. Peak boredom. I should have gone out today, but I didn't care enough. I should probably call my neurologist but I don't. Not yet. How miserable do I have to get before I ask for help?

I miss my kid, but I try to give her space and not call every day. Smother mother. Before she left, she showed me a new game on Roblox called Head Destroyer 9000. The colors of the game are super Pride flag and '80s neon, and you move your little avatar around to various stations in which you can get your head crushed. There's no blood, just a countdown, the head smash, and then you emerge from a station with a narrow or squashed flat head. After a few minutes of frantic running around, your head pops back into shape.

"That's it?" I ask her. "It just smashes heads?"

"Yeah," she says, aligning her avatar, which has short shorts, wings, and a side-pony bouffant today, into a head-smashing station. "Wait for it."

And I do, and it's deeply satisfying.

I both do and don't want to make a big metaphor out of this game. It is just quite pleasing to destroy yourself for a moment in a game in which you are both you and a pixelated version of you. Cartoons allow for so much of this kind of smashing, but not self-smashing. Gen Z and Gen X really align. The pointless smashing of it all.

But it's also like 2020. When you think you can handle the next thing, there's killer hornets or fucking white supremacist cops murdering George Floyd by kneeling on his neck. At a protest you sing "Happy Birthday" to Breonna Taylor and you start to cry, because what is America planning on doing about the legacies of slavery? She should be alive and eating an amazing cake. We shouldn't even know her, because she got to live. And of course there's COVID, which never ends, and you can't touch anyone unless you're already partnered or your germ bubble didn't desert you, and it ALL DESTROYS THE HEAD. 9000. And then your head comes back and you do something. Tomorrow, I hope to leave the apartment.

## BUNNY

I join another protest with Lana at Stonewall for #BlackTransLives-Matter #NinaPop #TonyMcDade. All queer people, Black queers and white queer allies, and in the park across from Stonewall, we listen to the stories of our Black trans siblings and why they are here today and what they need from us and America. Basics that are the hardest to come by in this country: free medical care, dignity, respect, love, money, being able to #WalkWhileTrans and use the bathroom of their gender. Mostly they want to live and be left alone.

At every protest I've been to these last two weeks, there are activists moving through the crowd offering masks, hand sanitizer, fruit, nuts, protein bars, water, tampons, and homemade kits in baggies with all of the above. This level of care among activists doesn't surprise me. I know the caring of Occupy and Black Lives Matter, and I've been coming to this park for the last couple months, just sitting here and watching queer elders talk with younger queers, and share drinks and french fries. Still, I hope the world knows how marginalized people have been caring for one another for centuries.

I come to this march with one of my favorite former students and her girlfriend. They are very cute together on Instagram and IRL, and protective of me, which I don't mind.

"Are you comfortable? Is this a good spot for us? Can you see?" my former student asks.

I nod a lot because it's hot and the effort to talk through my mask is wearing me out. We march through the park and out into the street in front of Stonewall. Behind me I see my friend Bunny and her lover, Memphis, and I squeal. We make air hugs at each other. I haven't seen Bunny in months and Memphis in even longer, and they are dear to me. Another former student who helped me come out with her wisdom around pansexuality is also right next to us.

"I haven't been outside in three months," my former student says. "And this is my roommates' first protest."

We are a little hub, a group, a gaggle, the podcast *Nancy* would say, for a queer group of friends.

"Bunny, Bunny," I say. "I wish I could touch you. I'm so happy to see you."

"I knew this would be good for you," she says to me. Bunny, who is younger than me, but really my queer elder, the woman who told me to write about my queer self, to be out on the page and not just in bed. Bunny of the beautiful long fingers and deep astrological wisdom.

"Our hair!" I say to Memphis because we are both growing mullets. There is nothing to do with hair but wait, allow it to go feral, and for me, gray.

As we chant and dance, the crowd surges and pulses with a queer joy that is so different from mostly straight marches. There's a banner hanging over the Stonewall Inn entrance that says "Stonewall was a riot!" and we scream as we pass it.

I remember the one time Eurydice and I went to Stonewall. As we sit at the bar and order martinis, her hair falls over her eyes and I kiss her hard and long because I can. It's Stonewall and nobody fucking cares.

"Babe," she says. "Babe, you're making me wet."

"Good," I say, and settle back onto my barstool.

We start talking to the man next to us. His name is Faustus, and I shit you not, it turns out he's a professional jouster for one of those traveling medieval shows.

"You are *not*," I say, flirting because he's a man and Eurydice is a woman and they would make a perfect sandwich around me.

"Do you want to see a video?" he asks.

We nod and then watch him, dressed as a knight, fake joust with another man dressed as a knight, both on horses, while the crowd goes wild.

"Our very own knight in shining armor," Eurydice says, flirting now too, either for my sake or maybe because she's also attracted to him? She's told me she likes to cuddle with men but is very proud of her gold star status. I hate gold stars for any behavior and gold star lesbians are annoying, but I tolerate it in her because I love her.

An older fellow at the other end of the bar buys Faustus a drink, and we lose him. Later, we go up to the dance floor, and for one hour there's magical dancing, because it's lesbian/bi girls' night and the DJ is really good. I'm not sure I can articulate the utter joy of fifty queer women shaking their asses to Britney's ". . . Baby One More Time" and TLC's "No Scrubs." My joke about "No Scrubs" has always been that I love scrubs and that guy "hanging out the passenger side of his best friend's ride" has always been my type of dude.

Eventually I see that Eurydice has had too many drinks. She's an amazing, athletic dancer, and she's doing drops and moves around me that make me think I might fall down, because while I'm cute on the dance floor, I can't do moves. Choreography eludes my disabled self, though I suspect if I ever had a patient, kind teacher, instead of a huffy, bitchy straight girl trying to teach me, I might have succeeded.

Remember, I am a spaz. But there is some kind of rhythm that takes over me that helps me dance and makes it fun and nice for me. Another girl is dancing with us and it seems like there's a competitive vibe between them for me? or for each other? which I can't figure out and I start to feel bad. Those two are drunk. I'm a little buzzed, but mostly alcohol hurts my muscles.

So we leave and have a fight on the street that makes no sense to me.

"You're hot and I want to show you off," she says.

"I can't dance like that and if you dance around me too closely I lose my balance and I can fall."

"That girl wanted you," she pouts.

"I really think she wanted you," I counter.

Around and around until I say, "Enough, you're drunk, let's talk about it in the morning." At my place I tuck her in because I'm an enabler and I look at her while she sleeps. She's so pretty. She's so handsome. She's a mess. I'm a mess. "You're lucky," I say to myself, and press my butt up against her.

"Babe," she mumbles at me in her sleep and pulls me closer.

That touch I once took for granted. People in beds pulling me closer to them. Someone, her, calling me "babe." A crowd of queers dancing and sweating on one another in a club. Will we ever have that again? I wonder if Eurydice is somewhere at the protest today. I have a desperate wish to see her, because I think if she sees me she will remember that I'm human and worthy of connection. That I'm not just a ghost.

I turn around and search for her lanky body and poof of wavy, brown hair. But I don't see her. I look back and she's never there. Stonewall falls behind me too, or for a second I have a vision of that place in its older, darker, hidden time. When queens like Marsha P. Johnson and Sylvia Rivera ruled the space, the drinks were watery, and there was just a jukebox for dancing. What if the new Le Monocle is hidden inside of Stonewall? Or maybe it's in someone's apartment and we'll all be given rubber suits before we're even let in.

The crowd moves, turns onto another street. I maneuver Lana, but she's getting heavy and I know that the bikes should go to the side or back. My knees are starting to ache and I tell my friends I have to go.

Later that night on Twitter, I see that cops attacked the protesters. Bunny texts me that things got violent and they had to scatter.

"There were easily five thousand of us. At least that's what I heard a cop say."

"I love you," I text her.

"Love you too, Raccoon," she responds.

One of the protesters, writer and activist Jason Rosenberg, reports that the cops beat him so badly he broke his arm and needed six staples in his head.

The cops won't or can't stop themselves.

*WEEK SEVEN*
*JUNE 14, 2020*

# ARCHIVES

Many of my favorite photographers—Brassaï, Arbus, Touchette, and lately John Edmonds and Heji Shin—reveal hidden worlds or worlds overlooked by the white, straight, or able-bodied gaze.

At night before bedtime when I am often the saddest, I look at photos by Brassaï and watch documentaries that are part of the Netflix Pride series. This week I watch *Crip Camp, Circus of Books*, and *A Secret Love*.

I reopen my Lex account and write to some people to see if anyone will write back.

The Brassaï photo I keep returning to is awash in black, white faces emerging from the dark. Either very butch or very femme. Butch is a tuxedo, bowtie or necktie, sometimes a vest, short hair parted on the side, and the monocle, which in 1930s Paris was queer code. The femme women have set wavy hair, silk dresses, bare arms and shoulders, stockings, lipstick, plucked, arched eyebrows. Cigarette smoke lingers in the dark. What pulls me, pricks me, shoots into my heart like an arrow—*the punctum*, as Roland Barthes calls it—is the couple dancing in the foreground. Their cheeks pressed together. The butch's lips pressed to the femme's cheek, whispering to her or kissing her. Hands clasped. Butch's hand on the lower back of the femme. Such intimacy. Such closeness.

In the documentary *A Secret Love*, we meet Terry and Pat, who have been together for sixty-five years and have come out to their families in the last three. These two—total babes even in their seventies—show me a kind of love I've not yet experienced. Long-lasting, partnered, enmeshed. There's video footage of them skating, swimming, playing, laughing, dancing, working. It feels like a retrieval. The archive of lost queers. A correction. Their style and glamour. Unlike the lesbians at Le Monocle, able to hide in plain sight.

During much of the filming, Terry, who is also a former shortstop

for the All-American Girls Professional Baseball League, is struggling with Parkinson's. It's a movement disorder, with some symp-
tom overlap with my own, and I know the pain it causes. And then
Pat is sick, and we see the two of them, Terry shaking next to Pat's
hospital bed, struggling to raise Pat's hand to her lips. It takes effort
and time, but she does it. Their conversation in this moment is so
intimate, maybe the language of the bedroom, which is hinted at in
photos throughout the movie.

*Such a good little girl.*
*Who is my sweet little girl?*
*Are you going to be a good girl and eat?*
*That's my sweet angel girl.*

This is when my lips tremble. Later, I can't sleep. All of the lost
utterances in queer spaces. Cheeks pressed together. Hands holding.
Whisperings, occasionally overheard, rarely recorded. I think of how
Saidiya Hartman's incredible *Wayward Lives, Beautiful Experiments*
achieves this too, another unearthing—this time of Black women
and girls from 1890 to 1935. Hartman writes of her project:

> The endeavor is to recover the insurgent ground of these lives . . .
> to affirm free motherhood (reproductive choice), intimacy outside
> the institution of marriage, and queer outlaw and passions; and to
> illuminate the radical imagination and everyday anarchy of ordi-
> nary colored girls, which has not only been overlooked, but is nearly
> unimaginable.

What a sentence! What a book! I don't know why I need to tell
you about these texts now, other than they are shaping me as I write
and ride. I'm logging into the autofiction archive. I bring solitude,
disability, illness, and love.

When I begin writing I am a girl with crayons and newsprint,
later with a diary and a small matching pencil, and for most of my
adult life, I write about girls and women. The girl is the forgotten
one, so easy to dismiss. But the girl is everything.

# POTHOLE

I try to keep up with the protesting cyclists, but they are fast. I spot them after four hours of protesting in which I held up the back end of the march with the other bikers. We block a police car with our bikes. A white lesbian named Kay bosses me into this job. I don't mind it, but she wants to talk a lot and I get tired pushing the bike and watching the cop car and listening to Kay. Whatever, white people problems.

Sometimes the cop car and I are side by side, and whenever I look into the window, I see a young white woman, hair in a ponytail, shoulders tensed over the wheel. She doesn't look back at me. Eyes straight ahead. This is something I hate about the police at these protests. The way they look past you, over your head, anywhere but your face and eyes. Or they have dead eyes, like you don't register.

My knees hurt, my shoulder hurts, my robot hasn't been working so I'm typing too much. Not taking care. I should go home.

But they whiz up Fourth Avenue, and I instinctively turn toward them and pedal hard. "Catch up," I say to myself. "Catch up."

They shout, "No justice! No peace! No justice! No peace!"

We take up the whole street and I pedal as hard and as fast as I can, but I'm still falling behind. I let myself slow down and slide over to the curb, where I rest my foot and root around for my phone in my backpack.

What am I looking for?

No one's texted me.

Check email. Check Twitter. Check Facebook. Check Insta.

More bikes trail past. I zip my phone away, check over my shoulder, and push forward. My weaknesses are everywhere: car doors, double-parked cars, and buses. Buses scare me. Also squeezing between a bus stopped at a light and a parked car. I'll sit in bus exhaust rather than do that.

I pedal west after them, toward the river. The sun is setting over the Hudson, gleaming onto Fourteenth Street and into my eyes. I can't see. I squint, slow down, coast.

"Whose streets? Our streets! Whose streets? Our streets!" the cyclists up ahead of me chant.

I see the pothole, really a small crater in the asphalt, for less than half a second. My reflexes are too slow, and so my front tire plunges down into it. I grip my handlebars tightly and stiffen my arms. My backpack flies out of my front basket and for some reason, I try to grab it. The bike turns to the right and into what I know might be traffic behind me. This is it, I think, I'm dead. The sun is still shining in my eyes as the tire lodges itself in the hole, and then a second later it pops out. Miraculously, I don't topple over. But then I run over my backpack. My lock, also in the basket, jumps out onto the road, and I run over that too. I feel the bike seat between my legs. It hurts. I stop. My legs shake and I get off the bike, pick up the lock and my backpack. I fish my phone out of the front pocket. It's cracked.

"Fuck," I say to no one, because the street is actually empty.

I press the home button. It works. Seemingly.

I walk my bike home. Legs shaking. Sore pussy.

# DARK TIMES

When I am falling in love with Eurydice, I worry that someone will hurt her. People fuck with her a lot. They say, "What are you?" when she drops off deliveries. Sometimes a creep tries to lure her into his apartment.

"Just come in for a second. I gotta hunt around for your tip."

"I'm fine out here," she says.

One time, she loses her phone and I don't hear from her for two days, and I'm sure she's dead. I text her one friend that I know, and she says, "Haven't seen her, but I will ask around."

Eventually she shows up sheepish with no phone, crying. "I tried to see my kids and my ex wouldn't let me, and then I went to Cubby and got so drunk, they threw me out." I say a bunch of useless, angry things about her ex, and she sobs. I feel terrible when she cries, and I cry too.

"Trans women still lose their kids, you know," she says.

"I know," I say stupidly, uselessly.

I feel like she leaves parts out of the two-days-missing story, but I don't press her. I just say, "You can tell me anything. You can also have secrets."

She falls asleep for twenty-four hours, wakes up with a fever, and I beg her to go to Callen-Lorde.

But she won't. We wait it out, and then she wakes up after another half day as if nothing happened.

"I don't want to talk about it, babe," she says. "I want to live in the moment, with you."

I nod, something lodges in my heart, and I ask her if she wants Taco Bell, her favorite. "My treat."

Gina carries a knife from when she was in Iraq and so I worry less about her. But I don't think it's good that she won't leave her house, and sometimes I know it's fear that keeps her inside too often. She says she doesn't want to get "clocked" or read as trans, and Picasso worries about this too.

Picasso doesn't acknowledge very many people, but I see the way people look at us in certain places. They are trying to figure something out. One day, before the virus, he says to me, "If I have to go back to Brazil, I will. If your country doesn't get it together, I can do that."

Is my middle-aged, white, cis face protection? Likely.

If you love trans people, if you have trans friends and lovers, you worry because of what can happen. Just like you worry for your Black and Brown friends, because America is so violent and racist and it's a dark time. Or you worry for yourself and your family because you are Black, Brown, Asian, queer, trans, and/or disabled.

This book is set in a dark time, a changing time. I can't always keep up.

*WEEK EIGHT*
*JUNE 21, 2020*

# GOODBYE

I wake up still sore from the pothole and look at my cracked phone. I dread having to pack, but I've found an apartment.

I get an email. "You've passed the first round for inclusion in Le Monocle. In a day we will send you instructions for an address in Brooklyn where you will have an interview."

I wander around my living room in the midst of all my half-packed boxes and garbage, and daydream about touch. A hand on my ass, an arm around my shoulder, someone spooning me or me spooning them. I'm not sure I even want to have sex anymore, just touch, companionship, some people together in a room, maybe hugging or dancing forehead to forehead or cheek to cheek. I'd like to sit on my couch with another adult and watch TV. I'd like someone to cook a meal with me or for me. These are the thoughts of single, disabled people ever since we got the autonomy to live on our own. We want dignity and we want companionship. The fact that the abled world is just experiencing the need for companionship and care in new ways is not lost on me. It makes me furious actually.

I take a break because my shoulder throbs from the packing. Why do I have so many books? How have I accumulated so much stuff? My kid is a garbage collector and so I am!

I walk out the door of my building and into the park. The lamps are on, a few people sit far from one another on benches. Maskless skater boys *clack clack clack* against the Garibaldi statue. "He united all of Italy!" my kid used to say of that statue when she was six. She loved that he carried a sword. I think of all the statues that must fall, and that he is probably one of them.

Activists and homeless kids sit in the fountain. The fountain has always belonged to them, and rightly so. Someone is playing a guitar, and the mood is festive, hopeful, determined. There's no water this year because of COVID, and so the center is a kind of stage. Two teenage girls hug on the little stage, and I'm so happy for them, that they have each other, and get to touch. Maybe they're a couple? They have matching cat-whisker masks.

I circle the fountain a couple times, trying to take it in, to say goodbye. The way the cloudy, blue-black sky peeks through some of the trees. That underneath us is Lenape territory, a community called Sapokanikan, and a waterway called Minetta Creek, which might have come from the word *manette* meaning "devil's water." The Dutch stole the land from the Lenape, and in 1797, New York City purchased part of the land and turned it into a burial ground for the homeless, poor, criminals, and victims of yellow fever. There are likely twenty thousand bodies buried in the park.

Goodbye, Lenape. Goodbye, people who were buried here. Goodbye, fountain. Goodbye, activists.

I walk to the Hangman's Elm, the big tree on the northwest corner of the park where the dealers hang out. They are busy talking but take the time to say to me, "Smoke, smoke, smoke." I shake my head and keep walking outside of the park and then back toward my building.

The last person to be hung in the potter's field was Rose Butler, a nineteen-year-old slave, who set fire to her owner's residence. No one was hurt and only three stairs were damaged, and still she was hung. There was also a free-Black community nearby called Little Africa, and so I consider how close she was to freedom. Rose Butler sounds like a revolutionary to me.

When I get home I lie on the couch and ignore the boxes. I think about the histories I've lived on top of for these last eight years and how I don't want to walk on a grave site anymore.

I miss my kid, who told me she didn't want to say goodbye to the apartment and the park. "Mama, you do it. You say goodbye for us. Just pack and take me to the new place. Otherwise I'll get too sad."

What is the land—native territory, a cemetery, a public space, real estate? Right now, in these protests, we need to unearth it all.

What is a mother but a receptacle for holding feelings? It's one of the best things I do actually—as a mom, a teacher, a writer. I try to make and hold the space for us. On a couch, in a room, on Zoom, on social media, in essays, poems, and books.

Collectively, I say to you, "This is so hard. I love you. Don't give up."

# A CHRISTMAS CAROL

When I'm in third grade, I go to the hospital in Buffalo for a week. My parents visit but are mostly two hours away in my hometown. I am miserable and convince myself that they are going to lose me, that I am trapped in the hospital, that I can't leave. I am there for a week. I cry a lot. Painful tests. Boredom. Bad communication. The worst thing is the spinal tap, which makes me so sick and freaks me out because I don't know what's happening.

The night before I'm supposed to be released, the nurses take us to a production of *A Christmas Carol*. It's December, snowy cold, the van's heat isn't working, but we get there. All the orderlies are these sweet Black men with Afros who carry us around and cover us in blankets. I think of *Crip Camp* and the intersections between Black counselors from the South and crippled white kids mostly from the city, and that when disabled people occupied the Health, Education, and Welfare building in San Francisco to protest in favor of passing 504, the Black Panther Party fed the protesters every day.

The play is special. I feel it. Remember, I am Tiny Tim. My cuteness as a sick child is a consistent comment. This pretty-little-girl thing and my good-patient behavior probably get me more treats and cookies and doctor love. I will do anything for the love of a good doctor. I want to be cured. I want to be better.

I won't write about what happened with the pervert orthopedist in the basement. Right in front of my parents, who had no idea. I won't write about him. I am trying to get up the courage one day to request my childhood medical files. There are videos. So much paper. I was a rare specimen. I started the paperwork a couple years ago, and then didn't follow through with the last step to have them mailed. I didn't feel ready, but I didn't want them destroyed. I still want the videos and to see all my misdiagnoses and what my doctors wrote every time. What their interns wrote. Maybe after I publish this exorcism, I will be ready. I am afraid of what's in there. Afraid to confront that sick little girl.

Onstage there is snow! And a flying bed! The theater is dark and warm, and it's a couple hours of pure hospital escape. Art. Ghosts. Chains. Redemption. The wicked turn good. "God bless us, every one." Tiny Tim takes a couple feeble steps. I don't feel sick in the dark. Like I'm released from my hospital chains. The sound of the chains onstage is especially terrifying and real. The theater falls away and I am in the play. The best theater does that.

One of my most terrible bosses was a Dickens scholar. He made my life and my colleagues' lives hell for over ten years. He was rigid, cruel, and cheap like a Dickens villain. He encouraged and ignored the racist, sexist harasser who eventually tried to destroy four of us in court. But we won. The Tiny Tims won.

I have a new boss now. I love her. She's a scholar of Eastern European social movements for change. She praises good work and protects faculty. She's sensible, never mean. I'm not sure she belongs in any Dickens novel.

When I pitch this book to Feminist Press, I draw on the history of serialized novels. Dickens was the first! He published all of his novels in serialized form. Also *The Woman in White* by Wilkie Collins and *Middlemarch* by George Eliot. I fucking love those novels. *Crime and Punishment*! *The Portrait of a Lady*! *Fear and Loathing in Las Vegas*! Armistead Maupin's super queer *Tales of the City*. And now *Panpocalypse*.

The serialized novel must move quickly and keep readers in suspense. It's also created as it's being read. I'm not that much further ahead of you readers. I like this challenge.

The next day when I leave the hospital, I am allowed to go to the gift shop. I am obsessed with the gift shop, with its stuffed animals, postcards, balloons, and little old ladies who work there. My dad buys me my first diary. When I get home I write in it. It's small and has a matching pen, and a lock I think is cute but don't much care about. The key is so tiny and it has a little ribbon string to keep it close to the diary.

My parents ask me to read from it at dinner that night. Of course, I do.

# REST IN POWER

On the fourth anniversary of the Pulse shooting, during Pride month 2020, the Trump administration moves to remove civil liberties for LGBTQ and disabled communities. He specifically targets trans people and their access to health care.

I sit on my couch and check in with my people: Gina, Picasso, Eurydice. Gina and Picasso say they're okay. Gina says her insurance won't change and her surgery will go forward, although it has been delayed for months because of COVID.

"I don't expect anything from those bigots," Gina texts. I miss her and wish we could cuddle, but in some way I know whatever we had is ending.

Picasso texts, "Thinking more and more about my people in Brazil and where it's safer."

Eurydice doesn't text back, and I begin to worry all over again that something has happened to her. Maybe this will always be what I do with her.

I make a list in my notebook—as an act of solidarity and mourning, a witnessing, moving from what I can find online to my head, through my hand, and down onto the paper—of all the trans people who have been murdered so far in 2020.

I sometimes tell my students that we learn more deeply when we write, and research shows this to be true. Note-taking by hand, freewriting by hand, anything going from a source into your brain and out your hand, is a learning mechanism. I am trying to learn by way of this sometimes-shaky hand and report back to you.

I take Lana out at night. It's Pride weekend. I keep forgetting that. There's a drunken dance party in the park across from Stonewall. I circle a few times before going in. A sweet drunk man starts talking to me, his mask down around his chin. I get it. The masks are exhausting. He's very close. Is he flirting?

"I want to see your face."

"I want you to put your mask on."

"I can see your body." He looks me up and down and I know I'm going to have to leave.

"How old are you?" he asks.

"I'm old, I'm forty-seven."

"You're not old, you're just dealing with some old shit."

I laugh through my mask. The brilliance of a drunk queen.

"Happy Pride!" I say, and ride away, loving how Lana gets me in and out of places fast.

I'm getting used to my mask life. It's easier for me in some ways. To be protected. I worry for the maskless men in the park, but it's their choice. I'm not going to tell queer people what to do. Straight people, now that's another story.

The sun is bright in my face. I keep riding in circles, around and around the West Village. I am going to miss it. This place of amazing, disgusting privilege, and queer history. The place where I came out. How important Stonewall has been to me. Mostly outside of it, but knowing what happens there. Christopher Street.

I cry on Christopher Street. Empty storefronts and Pride flags. The sex shop I never got the courage to go into and the crystal shop I love. The glistening Hudson at the end of it. The piers where so much happened. Ruins. Redone. Still queer though. In spite of gentrification.

In less than a week, I will be gone.

*PART 2*

*SICK TIME*

# THREE GHOSTS

In *A Christmas Carol* there are three ghosts of time. Past, present, and future. None of these tenses know if I'm alive. People say first person is the most unreliable narrator. I say it depends on the narrator.

I fall and fall and fall and fall.

"It's dark," I say. "I hurt," I say. "Am I alive?" I ask the darkness.

Past ghost rattles her chains, wears a stinky dress made of rags and plastic bags, and flies in on a broom. She yanks me awake, pulls on her chin whiskers, and carries a wand made out of baby bones. I see tiny femurs and a small skull on top.

"Come, come, now, don't delay," she says, and we fly off on her broom. I clutch her like she's butch and has a motorcycle. Her whiskers feel soft to the touch, but she shoos my hand away.

"Look down," she says.

"We're not even going to land?"

"You can see what you need to see. I don't have time for landings."

Through the clouds, a small parting, a cleft of vision, and me and my little lame self, running after all the girls in my clogs. They are not chasing me, I am chasing them, and then boys are chasing me. A long train of kids chasing the wrong kids. Because I couldn't run very fast and sometimes not at all, a boy catches me, pins me down, and plants a wet, slobbery kiss on my lips. I squirm and hate him, but he only gets off when he's ready.

After that, past ghost dumps me in my hospital bed. There are beeps, too much light, and nurses just like when I am little. Never a doctor. Never anyone who can tell you what happened to me. *What is wrong with her?* You are not the first to demand this.

Every disabled person knows you don't want to get stuck in a hospital. You want to be free even if you need help. You want to live with independence, dignity, and managed pain care. You want doctors to not fucking gaslight you and insurance to not make you suffer through their bullshit paperwork, and that's if you even have insurance. You want people to not say stupid shit like "You're so brave" or "You're such an inspiration." You want to be sexualized, seen as sexy, and have sex. You want the abled to know that, actually, disabled people are really good at sex because we've had to learn how to do things differently. We are magical, actually, so fuck off.

I remember my hospital girlfriend and hospital boyfriend. My roommate, who is dying of cancer, who has a mom that stays with her in the hospital, and in some ways becomes my surrogate mom because my mom is always working. Why is my mom always working? That is a question that can be asked of all working moms and is almost never asked of working dads. Still, I am ten, and ten-year-olds want their mom. It's a primal animal thing, to need the mother. That was a time when your mom wasn't the "good enough" mother, as D. W. Winnicott says. You only have to be good enough, you don't have to be *really* good, or excellent, or perfect. But given how few shits this country gives for moms, even good enough is challenging.

My hospital girlfriend wears a handkerchief on her head. Mostly, she turns away from me and falls asleep because she is exhausted. She's so pretty and delicate. She is my manic pixie dream girl. Or maybe I am hers. My hospital boyfriend lives down the hall. I skate in my hospital socks down the slippery floors. He's got a heart condition, but is alert like me. Ready to play games. I may have made him up. But the girl, the girl is real.

In the present, now, there isn't a ghost but a cat who swishes around our new apartment and stares at birds out the window. "We like it here. We like it here," the cat says. She sees the top of a hospital from our window, but she won't say if I am there. If she were to have her own bike like the cat in *The Master and Margarita*, she would fly it to the hospital and look for me, but you know about the pandemic. You know about the plague. When I ride around the new neighborhood, I whiz by the abandoned hospital buildings. The ones that look like asylums. The ones from another era, with boarded-up windows. We all know those are haunted with violence and transgressions. With sadness and longing.

The cat flies me to Willowbrook, to see what once was there. We're on our surrealist bicycles, crossing the Hudson, waving at the Statue of Liberty, and hovering over the asylum's abandoned buildings, the ones I've seen in the footage from *Crip Camp*. A young Geraldo Rivera uncovered it. This cat houses the memories of this place now in her brain, paws, and tail. Animals know so much, if we can only just listen.

We circle the moon and then hover down to the grounds. Tags cover the buildings now, and weeds and grass have taken over the concrete and bricks. All living beings return to the soil. Dust to dust. Ashes to ashes. We all fall down.

I see naked patients, too many confined to one bed, babies who long to be held, looking desperately at the camera, men in soiled diapers sitting at tables with nothing to do, a lone nurse's hand feeding gruel to a desperately hungry girl, women left alone in dark bathrooms to be experimented on and assaulted. Patients' arms and legs folded and bent in pain because they had no exercise or physical therapy. A man's head bloodied because no one stopped him from beating himself against the wall. At one time, there were over six thousand patients in a space meant to hold four thousand. A true Hades for the disabled.

When there are prisons, there will be abuse. My heart hurts to see it. My heart hurts to write it too. The heart knows what's wrong, and more than anything right now we need to listen to our hearts. The cat doesn't tell me what's in her fast-beating heart. She flies us back home and into our bed.

Many of us are just trying not to get institutionalized. To be free. #AbolishPrisons #AbolitionNow

The thing is, the gods are wrong to punish Orpheus for looking back, because if you want to save anyone or anything, you have to look back. You have to watch horrible things so you can know history and see the patterns, and not get tricked again.

The ghost of the future doesn't show up. She sends a text. She's tired. She can't make it.

"But what about the future?" I demand. She always pulls this shit. Such a fucking flake. "We were going to talk about that."

"Some people live and some people die," she texts back, and I seethe. She's the worst friend I've ever had and I vow to cut her out of my life. Once I can go outside again and touch people, I will not make plans with her. I will not fall for her offers of Aperol Spritzes, safely prepared by masked bartenders who practice social distancing protocols. I will not ride through Prospect Park with her and listen to her go on and on about Tinder and how many matches she has. "It's just so overwhelming," she will say, and I will not be there.

The cat purrs that I'm too angry. Of course I'm angry. I'm disabled and queer and lonely and sometimes it seems I will die without a partner as everyone has always prophesied about the disabled, and that's fine, but it's terrible when abled people are right because they actively de-sex us, shun us out of love, or pretend we don't exist.

I block the ghost of the future. *It's time*, I tell myself. *What is the future anyway during these days of panpocalypse? There is only the present tense.*

## BROOKLYN HAS PEOPLE, SKY

Dictating again. Is having a disability a series of hacks? Having to make do with what you can piece together. As I read *Disability Visibility*, I don't feel disabled enough, just like I never feel queer enough. Another thing I don't like about this software robot is that they won't type out swear words. Or learn the word *queer*.

Queer.

Queer.

Oh, they seem to have learned it.

What does it mean that I can walk now and ride a bike? What are the privileges of passing? Why have I decided to create my first disabled character?

In the last five years, I come out in all the ways. I aim to have no more secrets. I aim to be fully myself everywhere. I call this the "One Orpheus Mission." Also, I get sick again and I can't hide. I'm in so much pain that I have to talk about it. Doctors, my dean, my friends, my kid, lovers—suddenly, everyone must know.

What does it mean for me to have a disability community? What would it mean for me to have a queer community? Maybe I haven't earned community? I know I have friends, but COVID lays bare the limits of some friendships and the virtues of online worlds. It may be that I've forgotten what community feels like since lockdown.

I have a pain called Twitter neck. Do you?

It's phase two, the reopening, the reclosing. Yesterday, our president wears a mask for the first time. Over 100,000 people here have COVID.

I ride Lana to Williamsburg from my apartment in Prospect Lefferts Gardens, Brooklyn. It's 90 degrees and I take Bedford almost the whole way, into Bed-Stuy and then Hasidic Williamsburg. I sweat and sweat. I wear a polka dot sleeveless romper and Vans. Is this just NYC sweat or hot flash COVID sweat? I meet my friend

Jujubee for a masked drink. Berry Street is closed off to traffic, and we sit on the curb. So many people, so many friend groups, everyone masked. I can't stop looking around, because there are so many people and dogs.

"I met someone on a Zoom call," she says.

"What's he like?"

"I told him I got a pedicure and he said he wanted one too."

We giggle a lot from just one drink. Mine is called a mezcalrita.

"So he is not obsessed with masculinity."

"No," she says, and we laugh and laugh in the hopes that this could be true.

I am happy for Jujubee because we are both highly unsuccessful daters. We have mostly given up.

"I deleted all the apps," I say. There's no one and it's true. "Although I applied for a special queer club called Le Monocle. If you get in, you can touch people."

Jujubee raises her eyebrows.

"I know, I know," I say.

She's going away to a Hindu rebirth ceremony and I will miss her. Soon I'm going to Maine with my kid if state borders don't shut down. I can't take Lana and I worry about what that will mean for the book.

After our drinks, I ride in the dark mostly on Franklin, which is a beautiful street that I don't really know. A group of Hasidic kids play stickball in their old-timey clothes and I feel transported for a moment. One boy pouts on the sidelines and says with his Yiddish English accent, "Aaw da game in ruined."

So much pedaling, so much sweating. A dark passage. No people on the street, a smokestack in the distance. A man rides up beside me on a BMX bike and says something I can't make out. My heart beats faster in my chest and then he speeds past me.

I pass a string of restaurants and bars with outdoor seating. How nice it would be to go there with someone I love, a date. I'm not really sad anymore, just numb. I passed through some kind of withdrawal for skin, and now I don't remember what touch or sex feels like anymore.

The BMX guy is the closest I am to touch. When I get home I bring my bike inside. There's a bike room in my new apartment but I don't like to be away from Lana.

How lucky am I to not have COVID?

I watch Netflix documentaries:

*Athlete A*

*Cheer*

*Mucho Mucho Amor*

*Lenox Hill*

*Surviving R. Kelly*, which breaks me and makes me rethink uncomfortable things.

# MY PRIEST

Second grade, at Catholic school, where my atheist family doesn't belong but feels I will be safer—because I am very small, the smallest in my grade until high school. Because there's probably some racism about the local public school. Because the classes are smaller.

Each year I lie to the nuns. I lie a lot at this age. I do it for fun and to be left alone. I do it to avoid pity and to get people who wrong me in trouble.

"You're sure you were baptized?" Sister Grace of God asks.

"Yes, my parents don't really like to go to church, but they baptized me when I was born." This is a lie. I wear overalls and a plaid shirt with a Peter Pan collar, some kind of lace-up shoe. The priest, who visits our classroom sometimes, once called me a beautiful little girl. I think he's quite handsome too. Sister Grace of God is old and grouchy. She never smiles at us in the hall like some of the other nuns. Her habit is dark blue, with a white band around her forehead, and her dress is pale blue polyester. All the nuns wear this. Many of our teachers are not nuns, but mostly they are Catholic.

I think of my Jesus workbook, the story of the apostles. St. Peter and Paul, which is also the name of our school. I am learning how to take Communion like the other kids. I so badly want to taste the body of Christ and drink his blood.

"Do you remember where you were baptized?"

"Somewhere in California, where I was born," I say, waving my left hand in what I think is the direction of the West.

She stares at me, to break me. I squirm a little in my small wooden chair. I focus on Sister Grace of God's knees, which are in pantyhose. I wonder if hers come in the same sexy egg-shaped package as my mom's. There's also the Underalls brand, which is a cartoon of a woman's butt in her nylons. Also, unbearably sexy.

"If you've been baptized, you may take Communion in class. Will your parents have you participate in First Communion at a church?"

"Prolly," I shrug. "Can I go play?" I need to get out of there. Every morning as I leave for school my father tells me not to listen to the nuns, but it's an impossible situation. The nuns are in charge. My workbook tells me my family will go to hell. I don't want that for us, but my parents tell me hell is not real.

"Yes, you may go outside, but get your jacket and boots on," she says.

Outside, I see my best friend, Toast. She's both mean and nice. We're both kinda outsiders. She's poor and I'm a sinner. We sit by the swings because I can't run today. My legs hurt too much.

"You're going to burn in hell," she says.

"I know," I say. It's easier to agree with Toast.

A week later, we have our Christmas concert. They make us stand on risers, which I hate because one of my symptoms is that I can't stand still; I am always walking and falling backward to keep my balance.

I'm on the end of the second riser. The lights on us are bright and the gymnasium is full of parents on folded chairs staring up at us. In the back is a bake sale. I have made it to the last song, "Figgy Pudding," which we all sing with gusto because it's a song of kids and their demands and we like that. We don't get to demand much in Catholic school or in the '70s. I sweat and sing. I see my mom in the second row. I love her so much, and her face is looking at me like she's worried.

*Oh, bring us a figgy pudding!*
*Oh, bring us a figgy pudding!*
*Oh, bring us a figgy pudding and a cup of good cheer!*
*We won't go until we get some!*
*We won't go until we get some!*

The crowd starts to blur and the lights get brighter and hotter. I try to wrap my toes around the front edge of the riser, but there's no traction. My vision narrows to a point, and my face feels on fire.

The crowd gasps and the piano keeps going. The singing and my vision fade into a blur. I'm out.

I wake up backstage with my mom rubbing my forehead. "The priest caught you," she says.

"I ruined the concert," I say.

"No, but you terrified the parents," she laughs.

"Can we go?"

"Yeah, Daddy and your brother are waiting for us."

I walk out with my head down, my coat around my shoulders. I hear the whispers about me and get a few pats on the back. The priest smiles at me and I hate him.

The year I fall off the risers is the same year I begin to play doctor with a teenage boy who is my next-door neighbor. He's fourteen and I am seven. His mom is my babysitter. We go behind an abandoned house, take our clothes off, and look at each other. Sometimes we touch our butts together. I have been playing neighborhood doctor games with boys my age for some time. I suppose I like the control I have over them. Mostly, I make them do things and I do nothing for them.

"Run this brush over your thingie. Hard. Now harder."

"Take off your clothes and stand still. More still."

What I feel in these situations is that I have a powerful, wanted body, and I need this very much because everywhere else I have a pitied, ugly body, a body that doesn't work, that no one wants to touch, except real doctors and a creepy priest.

# SCROLL

July is #DisabiltyPrideMonth and I revisit Alice Wong's amazing anthology *Disability Visibility*. I wish I had this book sooner. I bet a bunch of us wish that and it's why Wong made it for us. Gifts. What a week. I stop writing because of neck and shoulder pain. The Department of Homeland Security begins kidnapping protesters in Portland. John Lewis dies. A fighter. A man beaten so many times. I cannot bear it.

I have a miserable day of solitude, maybe it's been five months of this now. I scroll and scroll and scroll until I want to die.

The center of my new building is hollow for recycling, and the super who has an office there. I take trash down to make myself stop scrolling, and follow a new corridor of sunlight. Overgrown weeds. One lone potted plant. Cement cracked. Trees overhead. A portal! I find a portal!! I think, *Garden!* We can make a garden club for kids and adults in my building!

I ride to the Nethermead and lie under a tree. I hug myself. Switch arms. Tight. Hug myself for as long as I can. The leaves feather and wave above me. A man starts doing yoga fifty feet in front of me. I copy him for a while and lie back down. I wonder if he'd have sex with me. Do I want to have sex with a cis man? Answer foggy. Try again later.

# ROCHE

In my late twenties, the drug company Roche stops manufacturing the synthetic dopamine I take large quantities of every day. The pills are chalky pink. Pure dopamine. They make me queasy and sometimes when I throw them up, the food I eat turns pink too. Pink hue. Pretty in pink.

I panic because I do not know the replacement drug and neither does my neurologist. I am sure this is the end of me. This life I manage to construct out of pills and pluck. I am supposed to get married to Guapo. He is worried for me, but also calm like Virgos are, certain we can figure this out.

Calm, like the day we went to get my first HIV test of my life. He'd had one, I wanted one kinda, but confess I have a wild fear from dating some heroin addicts and just being an all-around sex-positive slut that I must be positive, and living with the disease. My best gay friend thinks this for years too. I wonder how many queer sluts lived this fear-life for years because of the trauma of that era. Generation X kids like us, who grew up in the '70s and '80s, were taught that sex led to either two things: HIV positivity and certain death, or teenage pregnancy and the end of your life as you knew it. One of my favorite writers, Mattilda Bernstein Sycamore, is editing a book—*Between Certain Death and a Possible Future*—about queer people who grew up after the first wave of HIV deaths, but before there were any medical breakthroughs. In some ways, I've felt that queer and poly people have been better at negotiating risk during the pandemic than straight, monogamous people. A large claim, I know, but risk and testing have been stitched into the lives of queer people, and the force with which gay men in particular have been told that they would or should die would be astounding if it weren't so commonplace. What is it like for queer people to see the world mobilize around finding a vaccine to stop COVID, when we still don't have one for HIV? How many Americans have been willing to jeopardize the lives of Black, Brown, and immunocompromised people because they were unwilling to wear masks or didn't believe in them? There is a through line from the AIDS patients in the '80s who died alone, shunned by their families, and the COVID patients who died alone on ventilators, too contagious to see anyone but nurses and doctors. Maybe it's a map more than a line. Words and landscapes I might chart: asylum, hospital, risk, death, warehousing, borders, and disease.

Guapo holds my hand in the elevator when we return a week later for the results.

"I'm not worried," he says. "Because the test results don't matter. I love you anyway, in spite of, regardless of."

Guapo, what a good man. I wish I could have stayed married to him, but I hate being a wife.

The gay man who seems to be the entire staff of this university testing site is very kind.

As soon as I sit down, he says, "You're negative." I wonder then if he sees me as another silly straight girl who is terrified for no reason. Now I think he had the hardest job and was doing it alone. Now I see that I wanted him to know I am queer, that Guapo was one of many different types of men in my life.

I don't feel as much trauma and fear with the two COVID tests I've had, but I spend a lot of time lately thinking about labs, pharmaceutical companies, and testing kits. This feels like a queer disabled legacy, one I reluctantly claim.

Outside of Roche laboratories, Puerto Rican nurses protest with body bags.

Outside of the Department of Education in New York City, teachers protest with mock coffins and portraits of teachers who were killed during the pandemic.

How much protest speaks to protest. These protesters using the death theater of ACT UP. How protesters can become a kind of family. How queer people make their own families.

Guapo tells me he has two drinks outside with a friend—a Manhattan, then a glass of wine. He rides his bike home through the dark in Fort Greene, through a stoplight, and another and another, and then there is a corner without a light and he feels wonderful because he got to see a writer outside from a distance, a friend who made him a drink, and the thing Guapo and I have always shared, even though we are not husband and wife anymore, is love of community, love of friends, love of parties and fun. We have become a queer family of sorts.

He feels soaring in his heart, and then he wakes up on the ground and two men stand above him. They are good men and they help him up. This is New York City and we fucking take care of each other.

Guapo is dizzy and his face is wet.

"Do you have your phone?" one asks.

He can't find the words to say anything because his brain is not connecting to his tongue.

"Where do you live?" the other one asks. He's dusting off Guapo's backpack, and standing his bike up. The seat and handlebars are twisted.

"You're okay, buddy," the guy holding his backpack says, and finds Guapo's phone in the front pocket of it. "Is there someone we should call?"

A synapse fires and zaps through a neuron. "My girlfriend, Pauline."

The three men wait on the corner for Pauline to come. They give him tissues for his bloody face and keep him talking.

The next day when Guapo calls to tell me what happened, I cry because he has a habit of accidentally hurting himself when he is stressed and overwhelmed. We both do actually.

"You have to be careful," I say. "No more drinks and then biking." I don't admit to some of my own tipsy rides.

Nothing can happen to Guapo. We cannot allow that.

# SWABS

Sit on your hands, so you don't flinch.

Just a tickle.

You might want to sneeze, but try not to.

Just ten seconds.

At the Coney Island Hospital.

At CityMD on Fourteenth Street.

Three times at the ModernMD on Flatbush.

A self-swab kit on Fort Hamilton Parkway because all the other tests run out.

Two times at the CareCube by Guapo.

SARS-CoV-2-Antigen Fluorescent Immunoassay

Negative N

Negative N

Negative N

Negative N

Negative N

Negative N

Negative N

Negative N

I get tested so many times, I don't flinch anymore. I'm not afraid of the swab, and I'll wait in pretty much any line. I get tested and travel to Maine to be with my friend Diamond. I'm negative but I still quarantine for a couple days. In Maine it is not a morgue. No one seems ruined by death or quite as lonely as I've been. They make a pod with me and my kid. It's my first official pod, an opening up. Diamond is queer like me. My college roommate, a dreamer and a doer. Every summer she gives me hope.

She calls her husband "Daddy," and I want to call him that too. I call Guapo "Daddy" now. It's my all-purpose name for people of any gender who I feel can hold me in space safely. I had an occasional

Daddy like that growing up, but mostly he was depressed and angry. Watching *Surviving R. Kelly* nearly ruined that word for me, but I must have it back. He used it all wrong, to abuse and silence. Good Daddies don't do that.

I wonder if I will ever have my own Daddy or if I'm capable of giving off Dad energy? Outside of New York City I always feel more butch.

Diamond and her Daddy touch me a lot because I need it. A couple of times we make out in the kitchen and I feel lucky again, and a little bit like myself before COVID, but different too. Forever changed.

# ALMODÓVAR

I dream a whole Pedro Almodóvar film in which Antonio Banderas plays two roles—both leads—the old Daddy bear who is a successful artist and his young assistant. He is not as convincing as the younger assistant, but still quite good. There is an oldish magazine/newspaper office, which also happens to be my actual office, but with an open floor plan, and more light and hustle. Daddy Banderas keeps making passes, actually harassing assistant Banderas, who is clearly not into it and has morphed into Paul Preciado with a skinny mustache.

There is an uncomfortable cab scene and then we arrive at an art opening. Daddy Banderas is anxious and kind of hiding. The décor is lush with couches and gold rugs. Lavish. I realize this is his art. The crowd is catty and unappreciative of what Daddy has made. They whisper that his earlier work is better. Assistant Banderas tries to talk to the remaining guests about the older parties and Daddy is pissed and in need of assurances. There are reds and yellows like in all of Almodóvar's films. There are some good zines, which me and some dykes like. I have a bowl cut like on the day I learned to ride my bike.

The assistant announces he will not stay for the after-party. "That time has passed," he says. Daddy is feeling washed-up with his gray beard and lets him go.

There are some neon pinks and an older New York City when the rest of us go out. We want the Daddy to be happy.

When I wake up, I have a terrible neck ache. This dream movie has some overlap with the last Almodóvar movie I saw, *Pain and Glory*. But mostly it has doppelgängers! A word from the German. Literally "double-walker," a biologically unrelated look-alike or a double of a living person . . . In modern times, the term *twin stranger* is occasionally used.

I think of the Orpheus I am in New York City and the one I am here in Maine. They are twin strangers or I am a double-walker.

# BULLY

A bully will wait for you. I have several when I am a child because I can't walk well. I also have a few protectors, but they can't be with me all of the time.

Chase comes out of his house when he sees me resting on the curb or dragging my left foot up the hill we both live on. My house is three short blocks from our school, but it is a hard and long walk for me.

Chase is tall, white, Swedish American, likely Lutheran—"a good Christian boy," the old, white Lutheran church ladies might say. His front screen door leaps open and he jumps out onto his lawn. "What are you doing? You think you can just sit on peoples' lawns and curbs?"

I get up, ignore him, and start moving.

"You think just because you're a cripple, you can sit anywhere you want?" I think of myself as *Splendor in the Grass* and in my brain I call him a dick.

Around this time, I start to daydream about flying. Not high up in the sky, but low to the ground, hovering a foot or so above the ground.

Remember that little weirdo, the Great Gazoo from *The Flintstones*, the alien who hovered above Fred's shoulder? He was a kind of unconscious alien superego to Fred.

My flight was to be an escape from suffering, from walking, and from Chase. My flight was a wish for a wheelchair without asking for it.

# CHRYSALIS

I wake up back in my Brooklyn bed alone. It's the end of August, a rainy day, and I'm cold.

There's a big bug on my window screen, slowly inching its way across the netting. Large, iridescent wings, big eyes, and six legs. The raindrops land on the screen and cling to the bug's body. It's a cicada. I've never seen one up close and I marvel at its size and coloring. The pandemic is a thing you can cling to—so is a book, a kid, a body, or an apartment. What I wish to be is a chrysalis changing, moving, and flying. Perhaps this is my Gregor moment, when I become the bug, but instead of being stuck in bed all day, I fly away.

I take pictures of the cicada and get dressed. Heat up old coffee and look up cicadas online. They burrow in trees from two to seventeen years until they hatch into what are called "broods."

A day of endless naps. I fall asleep before my tween does, and sometimes she texts me in the middle of the night. This morning I wake up to "Mama, Black Panther died," and then a string of crying emojis. On Twitter, we are distraught.

All over Brooklyn, the cicadas hatch and sing. Their noise takes over the nights and my friends who I don't see anymore post pictures on Instagram of the full moon.

# LE MONOCLE BROOKLYN

I get a text from an unknown number: "Our committee has decided that you may come to our new underground queer space, Le Monocle. Please arrive with proof of your negative COVID status, wearing no perfumes or colognes, and the attached statement, signed, containing our rules for contact and consent."

I stare at my phone in disbelief. I thought this was just a joke, an email vortex I'd never hear from again. I'm sweating on the grass in the Nethermead next to Lana, who rests next to me, like my fallen stag. I have no plans. I never have any plans.

A second chirp from my phone. The address, farther down Nostrand. "The party begins in an hour. First come, first served. Reply Y or N to indicate if you will attend."

"Y," I text back instantly. A place to go with queers to touch, maybe. I cannot believe it. It's late August, the mosquitos are starting to land on my bare arms, and the sun is setting. I want to change my clothes, comb my hair, but decide against it. It's more important to get there, to get in, and besides, clothes are not clothes anymore. We all wear bike shorts, loose dresses, rompers, tank tops, and cut-off jeans. If anything ever goes back to normal, there are some things I won't change. I won't ever again wear tight pants that constrict my stomach. I won't dress up or wear lipstick.

I hop on Lana and we ride out of the park as the sun sets. My heart races and I sweat everywhere, but especially onto my bike seat. It is now the summer of "WAP" and everywhere I ride the song blasts out of car windows. I ride down Bedford and hear it from three different parked cars, vape smells coming out of their windows. I'm giddy. Finally, a song about the pussies that are always wet. Finally, a song for us whores.

The song loops in my head as I pedal and pedal.

I get to the address, an empty storefront with newspaper plastered over the windows, and find a place to lock my bike. There's a line, a socially distant one, but still a line. I feel my heart drop because I don't think I'll get in. I wait for an hour, watching someone leave and then another person go in. It's slow and hot, and I want to give up, but I don't. It's a lot like waiting in a COVID testing line, except far more queer.

Finally, I'm at the door to the storefront.

"What's your name?"

"Orpheus," I say, trying not to blink too hard. The person, in coveralls with the arms and legs cut off and a bandanna tied over their head and another one over their nose and mouth, crosses my name off a list on their clipboard and holds an electronic thermometer to my forehead until it beeps.

"Ninety-eight point nine," they say. "COVID papers."

I show them a photo of the most recent negative on my phone.

"You're in. Straight to the garden, mask optional, please review the rules when you get to the back."

I try not to run to the garden, but I sort of skip-hop.

When I step in, it's like I googled "Magical Queer Garden." The space reminds me of the community gardens I used to see in the East Village when I first moved to New York in the '90s. The concrete walls have been turned into mosaics. On one side there's a merperson made out of green, blue, and yellow sea glass, holding a trident, their hair a nest of shells, with faded surgery scars a few inches under their nipples. On the other side, there's the LGBTQ flag, also a mosaic, made with sea glass, bottlecaps, and broken pieces of old dishes. It reminds me so much of the Mosaic Man's work, I think it must be his. Near the walls, the grass is tall and full of wildflowers. The center of the yard has a concrete dance floor. There's a wooden bar in one far corner, and the DJ in the other corner. A small waterfall burbles into a pond along the back wall between the bartender and the DJ. They've strung up paper lanterns and Christmas lights. The dance floor is busy but not crowded. Wooden benches flank the entrance. I gasp and will myself to step forward. A butch lesbian I

111

recognize from Instagram who runs or used to run a queer story hour at the LGBT Center in Manhattan dances with her hands up over her head. The bass is loud and I can feel it in my heart. She smiles at me and I smile back through my mask. "Take that off," she shouts and I feel welcome, in a way I don't always feel in queer bars. Something has shifted maybe, in me? In all of us?

I slide my mask down around my neck and smile back at her. I point to the bar.

"Do you want anything?" I ask her.

"I'm sober, but thanks for asking."

I wade through the dancers and to the bartender. There's only about twenty of us in the whole space, but it feels like such a crowd. "Two shots of whatever you like and one for you if you want," I say to the cute bartender, trying to summon up swagger because even though the space is amazing and someone said hello to me, I am still nervous. Queer spaces always make me nervous—Am I queer enough? Do I belong here?—and I haven't been around this many people in months. *This is all you got, lady*, I give myself a little pep talk. *You gotta make this work.*

The bartender bumps shot glasses with me and I down one and then the other. My throat stings. *Fuck it. I hate shots. I love shots. I must dance.*

I force myself out there and try not to think of Eurydice, who was the last person I danced with. My heart still aches for her sometimes. I find the cute lesbian and dance near her. I'm happy to have company, but there is no electricity between us. Two people in wheelchairs roll out onto the dance floor and I feel okay. I dance my little dance, wiggle my butt as I do, as the people in chairs circle and dart. The songs shift easily from era to era, Kylie Minogue to Donna Summer to A Tribe Called Quest to Missy Elliott to Kendrick Lamar. The twenty or so people are Black, Brown, white, butch, femme, gender nonconforming, all ages, and unmasked. I dance and dance until my knee starts to hurt.

I close my eyes and dream about those walkers with the little seat for resting, and how much I want one. The long ride from the park down Bedford and onto Nostrand has worn me out. I think about how I cried one day in a drugstore long before the pandemic—I was with Gina, and pulled a flowery cane off the rack and practiced walking with it. Gina said, "Ewww, that's sad," and I knew then that we could never be together for real, like in a long-term way, if that's what she thinks about canes. Canes are sexy, useful tools. They are not inherently sad.

Eurydice once helped me buy a knee brace, put it on me, and then ate me out. Maybe that's why I love her so.

I open my eyes and see a cursive sign, beautifully painted and resting now above the merperson like a crown, that reads, "Le Monocle." The sign tethers me to something I can't name. Déjà vu? The past? Mine or someone else's? A time when queers had more spaces, but less visibility? All the queer bars I've missed because I came out so late.

Someone passes me a vape pen and I take a long hit. "Thank you!" I say to her, and when I focus my eyes I see that next to her is Eurydice. I stop dancing. She does too. The woman who gave me the vape looks back and forth between us.

"Oh shit, is this Orpheus—Carley—whatever her name is?" she asks Eurydice, and I hate her for acting like this is a joke and not my heart breaking again in a thousand pieces.

"'Whatever her name is'?" My head whirls from the pot, what a mistake I've made coming here—but still, it's Eurydice in the flesh, standing right before me. The pull is magnetic. I want to touch her, hug her, something.

"Hey," she finally says. Wavy hair flopping down over her forehead, cuffed skinny jeans, a button-down shirt with the sleeves cut off. All of queer Brooklyn has cut their clothes apart during panpocalypse.

"Hi," I say back.

There is an air-sucked-out-the-backyard feeling, a tethering that hasn't died, our attraction, our chemistry, I think, but I'm not sure.

"What are you doing here?" she asks, as if this is her very own pandemic queer bar.

"I moved back to Brooklyn."

"This is Hera, my girlfriend," she says, and Hera nods a bored *hey* at me.

I want to die, but what actually happens is far worse: I burst into tears. Hera actually rolls her eyes, and mercifully stalks off into another corner to glare at us.

"I meant to tell you," Eurydice says, not looking at me but down at the concrete garden floor.

My stomach feels sick, like farts and diarrhea. "Why didn't you?"

"I didn't want to upset you."

"But this is even more upsetting. To not know, to be totally blindsided. You said you were moving back to Long Island to try to be with your kids."

"I did try, but my ex won't let me see them until I get a three-bedroom apartment, which is never going to happen, and I met Hera online and we both got COVID and quarantined together and then we just kinda stayed together."

"Like, living together?" My eyes keep gushing water. I have no control over them. "But you said you never wanted to live with anyone."

"I didn't plan this. We just went for it because we didn't want to quarantine alone."

"I am happy for you," I lie, trying to pull myself together.

"Thanks. I'm happy now. You know, she's your age." As if on cue, Hera walks over from her corner, still glaring. "Can we go?" she says.

I know these digs. That she is twisting the knife. When we broke up, it was my age, it was my mental illness, it was her kids, it was total gaslighting and lies and then ghosting.

"You're such a fucking liar," I say. I no longer care about making a scene, about being polite in front of Hera.

"Why can't you just be happy for me?"

"Because you lie. All the reasons you said you couldn't be with me were lies."

"The truth is after I left you, I got my act together. Hera asked me to stop drinking and I did." Hera folds her arms smugly, and for a quick second, I feel she might punch me. The narrative she has about me—that I am the bad ex-girlfriend—is not the narrative I have about me.

"I asked you to do that."

"Stop, it doesn't matter now. Stop looking back. I want you to be happy too. Find someone here, look around, get out of your head." She takes my wrist and tugs at my arm, a gesture of intimacy, and then pulls me in closer. I smell her—something soapy and sweaty and perfectly her. "Have you been taking your meds?" she asks.

I yank myself away, my brain bright with rage. Because it is the worst, most patronizing thing you can say to someone on medication.

Hera shoots Eurydice a look, and even she seems to understand this is a too-much thing to say.

"Fuck you. Seriously, fuck you," I say, my legs shaking.

Hera intervenes and pulls Eurydice toward the door to the garden. I will myself to turn back toward the dancers and away from Eurydice and Hera. I need to move toward the crowd and not them. The woman I was dancing with raises her eyebrow at me, and mouths *Are you okay?* I keep crying and dancing, but I nod yes as if to make it so.

The song shifts to "Gypsy" by Fleetwood Mac and I feel I must spin. The pot has hit me with its usual intense force on my dopamine and serotonin. People spin and I do too. When I stop, I'm facing the exit and there's Eurydice looking at me like this is nothing, like she isn't the first woman I fell in love with. Like she isn't the one who helped me come out of the closet, finally. Like we weren't completely in love and planning a future together. Like she didn't tell me every day for four months, "I love you. I love you so much." I take her in for one last second—the shape of her nose, her thin, set lips, and her gorgeous eyes. I very much would like to come out of Hades now, these last eight months of panpocalypse, the seeming end of the world, and then I turn away again from her and back to the dancers. When I spin again, she's gone.

After a few more songs, I head to the bar and buy two more drinks. "Rough night?" the bartender asks me.

"That was my ex-girlfriend and she came with her new girlfriend, who I didn't know about. They live together now," I confess.

"You just found this out? Now?"

"Yeah."

"Well, fuck them, and here's to you, babe," she says, pouring us each another shot. We down them.

"Thank you," I say, my tears starting to dry up. "I appreciate your kindness."

"Sit at the bar with me, be our mascot for a bit." She pats the table and I sit.

My thoughts spiral:

*Why am I always the starter girlfriend? The things my lovers have done with their next partner that they refused to do or couldn't do with me!!*

*Buy an apartment!*

*Get married!*

*Have a baby!*

*Become monogamous!*

*Become poly!*

*Get sober!*

*Go to therapy!*

*I am the car you lease, but never buy. I have to figure out why I do this to myself. Why I participate in these dynamics!*

"I'm going to dance," I tell the bartender. "It's so surreal to be here, to be with people, I can't waste it."

"Get it, girl!"

The garden spins a bit, and the lantern lights blur. The crowd has shifted, new faces, and not the sweet lesbian from story hour anymore. I don't see her. I have definitely had too many shots, but I dance in my own little bubble, even though my legs ache.

# PORTAL POEM

When I look up at the merperson, they are waving their trident at me, and then there is an actual person with freckles and short hair like me, dancing toward me. Cap, trousers, a work shirt. Boy me. I look down, because I can't bear to look a stranger in the eye while dancing, and also because tonight is a lot.

"Hello," they say as we dance near each other.

I hope so much they don't try to couple's dance with me because I cannot do that. The coordination that takes. No.

"Hey." I smile. "I'm Orpheus, sometimes Carley."

"I'm Orpheus too, sometimes Charlie."

"Come on. Don't," I say.

"What?"

"You know. Be weird and creepy."

"How am I weird and creepy?" they ask, rolling the words around as if they are new to them.

"Never mind," I say, because I am very tired and I actually don't have the energy to explain or even dance. I want the walker chair, but the DJ shifts the song into '90s hip hop, and I keep moving. The other Orpheus stays close but not too close.

It gets darker out, and the moon comes into view. White orb in cloudy sky. The booze sloshes around in my stomach—it doesn't mix well with my SSRIs.

"I'm very sad," I slur to Charlie.

"I know," they say back. "Me too." There are just a few people left. "May I take your hand?" they ask. I nod yes and they do.

"Let's leave here?" Charlie pulls on my hand, rubbing their thumb along mine in a mesmerizing way. I haven't been touched in so long.

"Yes, let's go," I say. I wave to the bartender, who is a blur. The mosaics look like impressionist paintings now. They pull me out into the hallway and closer to them. I study them for a moment and make a joke, "Why are you dressed like a newsie?"

"What is a 'new-sie'?" they say, breaking the word apart, laughing.

"May I kiss you?" I say.

"Of course, what a silly thing to ask."

I press them against the hallway wall, and lean my whole body into theirs. They are warm and press back. Our lips slow and then fast, and I feel tethered again. They keep pulling me.

"My bike," I say.

"I have a bike too," they say, and they do and it's next to mine, unchained and from another time like their clothes and I think it's early Halloween, it's a costume, a prop, who cares.

"I'm not sure I can ride."

"You can, we will go slow, to a place in the park." They are already on their bike, doing little circles in the street around me.

"I can't get hurt or disappear," I say, a moment of sobriety. "I have a kid."

"Me too," they say. "I won't hurt you. Where we'll go is safe and even if it's far, you can come back easily."

"What?"

They ride close again to kiss me. "Haven't you ever wanted to run away?"

"Yes." I am breathless now. It starts to rain, soft drops on our warm skin. "But only for a little while."

"Come." They ride slowly in front of me and I follow. We take only quiet streets. There seem to be no cars tonight. We ride side by side like the Citi Bikers, but at lights we stop to kiss.

When we ride into Prospect Park, a raccoon lumbers in front of us, and whatever fears I have left are gone with the raccoon's bushy tail. He ignores us, isn't feral, and is on his own journey. I've always loved raccoons—their will to survive and their joy around food, even garbage. Their bodies remind me of my own, big butt and small, grabby hands and arms. I've read they've taken over parts of Prospect and Central Parks during the pandemic.

"Where are we going?"

"To see the new arch."

The rain has stopped, and the air is cooler now. I see it up ahead, the dark mouth of the Endale Arch, under restoration. "I've read about it," I say. "But it's not finished."

We park our bikes near the scaffolding. More kissing. Their tongue is soft and warm against mine. Chest to chest. I close my eyes. They pull me inside the tunnel, past the scaffolding and toward the middle where the moon can't get to us. It's dark in there. We run our fingers along some old stone and brick work and the new wooden panels. Rough and smooth. Rough and smooth. We kiss and kiss, and then in my head or in the tunnel—I don't know anymore which is which—I see a kaleidoscope of images. Short film clips, quick edits like my daughter makes for her TikTok videos, of all the people who have ever kissed in this arch before. Flashes of faces, lips, necks, mouths, hands pulling at hair and touching necks, arms resting on shoulders, hips, asses, and backs, collars from different time periods, hats, shirts, skirts, pants, dresses, aprons, parasols, high heels, sneakers, lace-up shoes, roller skates, Rollerblades, body after body after body, linked in time and space.

"Whoa." I stop for a second to steady myself, but the film keeps running. "Do you see that?"

"Yes," Charlie breathes into my ear. "Isn't it magical?"

"Yes."

"Say yes again."

"Yes!"

"Here we go!" Charlie holds my back tightly as if we are dancing a waltz. The wind howls through the tunnel and the rain starts up again, harder, pelting the stone roof. Dust and twigs fly up into the air of the tunnel and then there is light, light, light—from the sun, the moon, the desires of all of these people who have found each other together in this tunnel—smashed together, all of us now, in time, and out of time, bound with longing, secrets, problems, illness, plagues, joy, death, and birth.

Charlie puts their hand between my legs and rubs. I moan and feel the rush of blood to my pussy. They unzip my pants and put their finger deeper inside of me. Raccoon eyes cross in front of us. I am wet. And then the orgasm's dark rush of pleasure. Red, red, red, all around me, and then we are gone.

Somewhere else. Through the night sky and into a different one, like when the cat took me, like when I was with the ghosts, only this time with Charlie.

*My kid, my bike, Lana, my apartment, my life*, I think, but don't say.

## PART 3
## MY DOPPELGÄNGER

The chapters set in Paris are translated
from the French by Pauline Naquet

# WE WRITE TO TASTE LIFE TWICE,
## IN THE MOMENT AND IN RETROSPECT

Somewhere, I have a terrible headache. I sit up and look around. An old room—wooden desk, wooden stool, a gray, ashy window, and a bowl of ice-cold water next to the bed. Charlie breathes softly next to me in their long underwear. I'm wearing all of my clothes, my shoes carefully placed at the base of the bed. Have I been here before? I remember a cat-sitting job in my twenties for a lesbian who lived along the water in Greenpoint. She fashioned her apartment like this—spare, spartan, like it was from an older time, almost like a captain's quarters. I shake my head and my brain shifts in pain. I remember last night, the disaster of seeing Eurydice, the freedom of dancing, meeting this person, my doppelgänger, and riding off into the tunnel with them.

I go to the window and stare. A gray, rainy street, and a long awning reaching out over a café. Customers sitting and smoking with coffee and croissants. Not anywhere I know, but even after all these years there are parts of Brooklyn and streets that surprise me. But their clothes are formal, from another era, long and dark, and they are not wearing masks. The women are in hats.

I look around for my tote bag and see that it's folded neatly by the bowl of cold water. In it is my phone and the beat-up old Altoids tin where I keep my meds. I open it and they are all there—oval pink, big round white, little round white, and purple-and-white time capsule that reminds me of a space shuttle—so I feel safer. I slide the up button on my screen, but it stays black, which scares me.

Charlie sits up and rubs the sleep from their eyes. "What are you doing?"

"Making sure I have my medicine."

"For what?"

"So I can walk and not have a nervous breakdown."

"Medicine for walking?" They turn their head as if it's an impossible thing to imagine, and I suppose it kind of is. They smooth down the straw mattress next to them to beckon me over.

"Where are we?" I ask, clutching my phone to my chest.

"My flat in Paris," Charlie says.

"But how did we get here?"

Charlie shrugs and wrinkles the freckles along their nose. "I brought you to a time portal. Remember the beautiful tunnel and all of the people who had been there before us?"

"That's ridiculous," I say as my head throbs. Maybe this is it, I think, another psychic break. My teeth start to chatter. "I'm so cold. Why is your apartment so cold? Do you have a charger?" If I can charge my phone, I can sort this out.

"You kept asking me for a charger last night. We don't have those here, and that black box you're holding, I think you should just put it down, it's upsetting to you."

They are not wrong. Charlie pulls a scratchy woolen blanket on top of us. "When can I go back?" I ask as I settle into their arms and chest. They are warm, and it's so nice to be held. It's been so long since someone has touched me this way.

Charlie ignores my question, kisses the top of my head, and then my eyelids, which are closed now. I have so many questions, and yet I feel myself falling back asleep.

I feel Charlie's eyes on me. "I want to look at your face, the freckles are dazzling."

"They are the same freckles you have. Haven't you noticed that we look like twins? One boy, one girl, or one butch, one femme."

"I am a boy, but what's a butch?"

"A boyish, um, I dunno, mannish, I mean, masculine-of-center woman," I say, knowing I'm failing in all ways to do justice to the complexity of a butch dyke.

"So silly, these words," Charlie says, and begins to rub my forehead, the space between my eyes. I feel a return of the sadness I felt the night before, the weight of being locked up and away for so many months, the endless circling I do on my bike and in my apartment. Around and around because there is nowhere to go. I also feel the spark of connection with another person, something I haven't felt in so long. I've been aching for it.

Charlie keeps rubbing my forehead and holding me close. I wrap my legs around them. "Repeat after me," they say. "We write to taste life twice, in the moment and in retrospect."

"That's Anaïs Nin," I say.

"Who?"

"Never mind."

"Just say it."

"We write to taste life twice, in the moment and in retrospect," I say, as if I am reciting a spell or an incantation.

"Let's try this: America is my country, and Paris is my hometown."

"Stein?"

"No guessing." Charlie squeezes me and I giggle.

"America is my country, and Paris is my hometown," I repeat, and feel a small surge of patriotism or longing for home, my bed, my apartment.

"It takes a heap of loafing to write a book."

"Stein again. Why are you making me say these things?"

"Because it's fun and they are my favorite sentences right now," Charlie says, then kisses me softly on the lips.

"It takes a heap of loafing to write a book," I repeat, whispering into their mouth. Love Stein as I do, I do not think she understood the difficulty of publishing novels in contemporary America.

I kiss Charlie back, and we descend into each other. Mouths and bodies pressed together. Warmth. The room blackens at the edges of my vision, like an old photo burning up and curling when a match takes to it. I don't care so much that I am here or where I am, just that I am not in 2020 panpocalypse briefly. As long as I can get back to my kid in time for my parenting week.

I change the subject. "I'm writing a book," I say, and kiss them again. For some reason, I like people to know this, like I'm not just one person here and now or here and then, but I am also another person constantly taking notes in my head, keeping track, looking around. "Maybe you will be in it."

"I'm writing a book too and maybe you will be in mine," they say.

"What's yours about?" A pause in the kissing for writers to talk about their books, eye roll.

"The end of the world, or maybe the beginning, and a woman who gets a bike. What's yours about?" My vision is a pinprick now.

"Lesbians and gossip. May I?" They reach under my shirt and I lean into their hands.

"Do you have a kid too?" I ask, but I am not fully in the conversation anymore, because of Charlie's hands.

"I did, but my husband took him away from me when I fell in love with a woman. The judge was on his side. The whole town was, really."

"I'm so sorry." I press my forehead against Charlie's.

Their face is wet against my cheek. "It's okay. They will come to me when they are old enough and I will teach them how to be free."

We press harder into one another again and go deeper into each other's mouths with our tongues, like exploring caves, like learning a new cartography. Our hands run up and down each other's chests, and they are pulling my shirt over my head and I'm pulling theirs off too.

The tenderness I feel when I look at their binding. "May I, or do you like to keep that on?" I ask.

"Off is okay," Charlie says, and so I unravel them.

We slide out of our pants and kick them down to the bottom of the straw mattress. We are finally naked together, hands inside one another, eyes closed against the cold room—two bodies in their contours and edges, becoming one.

There are explosions everywhere in our brains, neurologists say. Synapses that fire and misfire. Dopamine surges. Serotonin leaps. The highs and lows of cortisol and endorphins. We chase drugs, alchemy, orgasms, spells, clarity, the universe, a vision of something larger than us, worker elves out on the far scaffolding of a galaxy, and most of all love and connection. We are humans who want to be gods. We are animals that long to be free. We are all babies who wish to attach and latch.

When I tell you we merge in that final moment of coming, I mean it. Two bodies became one in that bed. In pleasure, we resorted to atoms and matter. We broke time and space. If you want to think of the flux capacitor, go ahead, but it wasn't anything like that. It was my body into theirs and theirs into mine. It was the way, when we are at our best, as people, we become a collective, an organism. It was fusion without any fuss, and fucking for the win.

# MA PUCE

I wake alone in Charlie's bed, wearing Charlie's clothes. Standing up slowly, I go to the washbasin and mirror. My head still throbs. The water in the washbasin has frozen and the mirror is cloudy. I stare at myself. Boy Carley. Charlie. I was Carley and now I'm Charlie; both of us né Orpheus. I wear the work shirt, woolen trousers, boots, and long underwear that I took off of them—us—last night. Carley's clothes are folded neatly on the floor next to the washbasin. I wrinkle my nose at them—they are a snakeskin I have molted out of and left behind.

"Charlie?" I call out to the room that is really just this one room. "Charlie?" I say again. "Carley?" I try. Still no answer. I open the door and look out into the hallway—gray wood, and some beautiful metalwork on a railing, twisting down a spiral staircase. "Hello?"

No one answers. None of the other doors open. I go back into my—Charlie's?—room and wonder what to do for a moment. Do I need my medicine? Am I still my disabled self? If I'm Charlie on the outside, am I Carley on the inside? To be safe, I find my Altoids pillbox and slide it into the leather satchel hanging off the desk chair. There's a key hanging near the door. I lock up behind me, go down the stairs, out into the courtyard of my building, and into the street.

It's a riot of advertisements—for cigarettes, for shoes, for hats, for dresses, for Pernod, and for movies. There's a ragpicker and his wobbly cart full of garbage treasure. It's twilight, the lamps have come on, and I somehow know the way. As I walk, I forget most of the Carley things and remember all of the Charlie things. The way I walk is different too—all Charlie bounce and swagger, no more Carley hop and drag. For the first time in months, I am outside without a mask. I take a deep breath near a woman with two baskets full of baguettes, and hack. She frowns at me and waves me away, but before I go, I ask her what year it is, in French. I, we, Charlie, speak fluent French, but with an American accent.

"Bah," she says, disgusted with my cough and confusion. "It's 1935."

My lungs aren't used to this freedom of breath or 1935 Parisian air, which feels sooty and thick. She shoots me a last dirty look and wobbles her cart away. The streets are slick with rain and grease, and the cafés teem with people in smart hats, silk dresses, and beautifully tailored suits. How I long for a suit! My stomach rumbles, and instinctively, because Charlie knows how to do things here, I signal to a waiter and sit down.

He brings me coffee and I order soup and bread. The words pour out my mouth, quickly, though I can't shake my accent. The waiter takes my empty bowl away and brings me a drink that's cloudy and strong. In my satchel I find my notebook and cigarettes—arranging them on my café table pleases me. I wonder about my medicine again, do I need it here? I decide to wait and see. What if in this time, as Charlie, I am well? Looking over what I've written, I feel ready. For what?

The waiters begin to shift the tables around toward the back of the café. I move mine too so that I can see a woman in a slip of a black dress step onto a platform to sing for us. *It's my Dolly!* I think, though that Dolly belongs to no particular person. The song is cat-like, languorous, nothing I know, but she is perfect as a performer.

"I am your host!" She waves to a growing crowd, and I stand because I suddenly understand that I am meant to be on that platform, to read something from my notebook. "Don't you love these American writers with all their wild ideas?" Dolly smiles at me and then at the crowd. "Here at Ma Puce, we want to hear your stories and songs, you Yankees! Come, Charlie, come!"

The crowd roars for me. In New York, in 2020, I'm definitely not this popular. Their faces light up with wine and the glow of gaslight from the streets. Dolly's hand trails along my back and gives my ass a squeeze as she steps off the makeshift stage. Whistles and more clapping. I open my notebook, lower my cap over my forehead, and begin to read:

*On that ship, I outplayed the sirens and pleased Jason,*
*But then I was just an instrument, a boy without a subject,*
*A boy without a song of his own.*
*Some said I was a bawdy instrument, loose with notes*

Whistles, hoots, and foot stamping from the café crowd. Dolly smiles at me, her pretty, shiny teeth, her wet lips parted. I continue reading:

*And then I met my Eurydice, among the nymphs*
*With their braided hair and woven baskets.*
*She did ask to be undone.*
*She did walk alone among the weeds and wait for me.*
*And so we married.*
*But our bedtime was sweet and too short.*
*A snake in the night bit her and down she went.*
*I fooled that mad, three-headed dog to get her.*
*I begged Hades, and then I played for him.*
*Take her, he said, his black heart a little more blue.*
*But don't look back.*

Here I pause for the crowd. Dolly shouts, "Get her back into that bed and on her back!" I wink at her, and then at the front row of tables, which is all pretty ankles and shiny shoes. Oh, how I want a pair of shiny Oxford lace-ups!

*My love! The sun was bright and I wanted to show it to her!*
*I'm Orpheus, the poet, Charlie, the bawd, and it's my job to say*
*Look at that and look at this and look at me!*
*So I lost her, that maiden, that perfect slut, that wife of mine,*
*My first love, went back underground with the dogs.*
*On all fours, ma puce, on all fours!*

Dolly steps onto the stage and the crowd applauds and whistles. "Charlie! Charlie!" There's chanting and I walk back to my table. There are many drinks for me there, all cloudy and delicious, bought by fans, I suppose. I smoke and watch the rest of the performances. Each one a short, dirty, silly, mournful delight.

In Paris, I'm free. There's no plague, not for me. I write something silly and easy and perform it to cheers. I turn in my stories. I know what's behind me—the First World War, America, where I cannot be myself, my family who calls me a freak—and I don't know the future, but the now is exquisite, maskless, and full of people jostling and jiggling next to me.

By closing time, I can barely stand. It's me, Dolly, the waitstaff, the cooks, smoking and closing up. Dolly brings me an espresso and wraps herself up in a fur. I gather my notebook and cigarettes in my satchel and try to stand up straight. I down the espresso. On the street, it's cold. I am to jolt awake. I try.

Dolly laces her arm through mine. The street is quieter now. We pass sex workers in alleyways and Dolly nods hello respectfully. There are men asleep on benches, wrapped in newspapers to keep warm. "You were wonderful tonight," she says. I take her in, this beauty, this friend, this lover, this companion of mine. Her honey curls, her tawny skin, her rouged cheeks, her slippery dress, and her sheer stockings. She walks me down a series of alleyways, each smaller and darker than the next. I keep hold of her hand, until we stop. Two cats yowl and screech in the distance, and Dolly places my hand onto something—cold, perhaps rusty, I make out the shape of handlebars.

"Bikes?" I am so happy to touch a bike.

"Are you ready?" she asks, pulling the tangled bikes free from each other.

"Ready for what?" I say, though by now I know.

# ESCAPE

Dolly and I ride slowly through the late-night Paris streets, lamplit and shadowy. The cobblestones are slick with rain and garbage, and the bikes are 1930s bikes, slow and clunky, not like Lana with her many speeds. I have a flash of myself in NYC, pedaling fast, but it flickers like the streetlamps and is gone. The faces on the movie posters, bouncing stars in the dark, light my way: Claudette with her giant eyes, holding a goblet, pretending to be Cleopatra. Blond Annabella dressed as a peasant. Zizi with her gorgeous dancer's legs and gamine haircut.

I've sobered up on the ride and I remember what we're supposed to do. The hospital is next to the Seine, several buildings on a huge tract of land. There is a garden with a wall where Dolly and I are supposed to wait. When we get there, we lean our bikes against the wall under the leaves of an unkempt tree, and kiss to keep suspicious eyes off us. We are a sex worker and her client, lovers drunk in the rain, and nothing more. Between kisses, we talk. It occurs to me that there are some things I know and some I don't.

"You were once inside?" I ask Dolly, looking up to the top of the wall.

Dolly nods and lowers her head. "Yes. They experiment on you. There are some good doctors and nurses, and some perverts who mostly strike at night. If I escaped the asylum of America as a Black woman, I wasn't going to get stuck in some stupid hospital in France. When I left, I vowed to get as many people out as I could."

I try not to grind the back of my head into the stones of the wall. "I, me . . ." I pause, unable to explain to Dolly the doppelgänger I've become. "I've been alone in a hospital before, not sure when I would be allowed to leave."

"So you understand."

"A doctor once said to me, 'I can turn you into a man,' or, 'You must wear these braces on your legs,' or, 'You will have to stay here for tests,' and I had no responses. Here, now, with you in Paris, I don't think that way about myself—man, woman, neither is right. I'm Charlie. Orpheus. Carley. A person from the future who also lives in the past. A double. Like the two shimmering wings on the cicada of time. I would never let this man touch my body with his crude instruments again. I am two people tethered in time by a string of yarn. I am unfathomable and not for science. I am sick and I am well, disabled and abled, thrown into time and out of it."

Dolly looks at me. I've confused her. Perhaps she only knows me as Charlie. "You writing a poem again?" She laughs and then kisses me tenderly. "No matter, I'm glad we both got out of there."

I want to tell her I've escaped a plague in 2020 too, but I don't. My legs hurt as we wait. I doze off and suddenly see the orthopedist from my childhood, the man who made the leg braces that would deform my feet. Molded plastic with painfully high arches, and Velcro so thick and tight it left red welts along my calves. This was the same man who put his hands all over me while my parents looked on, completely unaware. In the rain, waiting for our escapees, I have fallen back into Carley's memories. Perhaps this is a thing that happens when I dream. Or perhaps I have a Charlie body and a hybrid Carley/Charlie mind. Maybe it doesn't matter. Two consciousnesses coming and going depending on the moment and what it needs. A shifting ratio. 80/20 Charlie to Carley, but 100 percent Orpheus.

I don't think the people who make most of these braces are disabled themselves because otherwise they would be made differently. Softer, less painful material, less stricture. Why does the disabled body need to be contained, shaped, molded, and controlled? To fit into the categories, structures, objects, and clothing of the abled body. A selling point of these braces was their clear plastic, so that they would be less visible, hidden perhaps in pants, covered by knee socks that fooled no one. Sometimes I wore them with skirts and I did not hide them. But still I begged my parents every day not to have to wear them. They forced my legs into painful positions, made walking and running more difficult, and made me more visible in public places.

My classmates never teased me that year. I'm not sure if there was a teacher's edict against it or if they genuinely decided to love me more because I was sick. One boy helped me with my braces when it was time to put our boots and jackets on. Another girl gave me extra Valentine's candy because she loved me so much. I was their Tiny Tim, a very sweet and cute girl they could get behind, though I didn't feel their care was secondary to who I was, mostly I felt helped and seen.

But elsewhere, things were getting very bad. Plenty of other kids outside of that class called me spaz and retard. A developmentally disabled boy whom I rode home with after school in a "taxi" threatened to rape me every day. It was the fourth grade. The pain was more intense than it had ever been. I took whatever kindnesses came my way.

In my dream the orthopedist stands over me and stares. "You'll need a shotgun to keep the boys away from this one," he says. My heart aches for my neurologist, a beautiful woman who would never treat me this way, whom I love so much, but who is the cause of my having to be here, or any other place in the hospital where she isn't. Her face, a shadowy mask, mouthing, *Kiddo, I'm going to cure you."

I am on a gurney being wheeled through a dark hallway by nurses whose faces are covered in PPE masks. There is the spinal tap, with the needles all over again, and the underwear they take off me without asking. There's my small, helpless child's body, underneath the bright light of a surgical theater, of a microscope, of a magnifying glass, like I am a bug to be examined. Some days they videotape me, which I hate most of all because it is performance of disability, an internist's eye refracted through the second eye of the camera lens. A double viewing, and then a record of my humiliating walk down the hallway without help.

I am always an object for examination. Spectacle.

When I get better, I refuse to be taped anymore. Start going by Orpheus, rejecting anything put upon me without my own permission.

Dolly shakes me awake. "My love, where have you been?"

"I, I—fell asleep standing?" I say, and then push myself to be honest. "I dreamed about a doctor who once hurt me, and the kids who made fun of me. I used to wear braces on my legs."

"Braces?" Dolly looks at me, worried. "My mother spent time in shackles."

I press my forehead to hers. "What a terrible country you escaped," I say.

Dolly shrugs. "France is not perfect, but at least here I can perform and work as I wish." She looks up at the hospital wall. "Where are they? Where are they? Soon it will be dawn, and harder to get them to Le Monocle."

Cats in heat howl into the night, and there's a glimmer of light at the seam of the sky.

"Where will we take them?" I ask.

"To Lulu, to Le Monocle, to start. She runs it and keeps a back room for hiding and all kinds of hijinks."

Eventually, a small rock flies over the wall and lands on the street, and then another. Dolly whistles to let them know we are here.

On the other side of the wall, breathing and whimpers. It's a high wall. Do they have help? Who will they be, these women, I wonder? I picture their white hospital dresses billowing like parachutes as they jump down to us.

First one woman and then another, on the top of the wall. No white dresses, instead they wear dark clothes—trousers and woolens they must have stolen or traded, and they've blackened their faces with ash.

I lean against the wall and make a ledge out of my shoulders. One at a time, they maneuver down to their stomachs, begin to slide down the wall and toward my shoulders, and then into mine and Dolly's hands. A dog barks madly from the other side of the fence and a light goes on from inside the grounds.

When we set them down, their eyes are wild with fear.

"You're free," Dolly says. "This is Charlie and I'm Dolly. We'll take you to a safe place."

One of the women begins to cry.

"Look how far we've come, Kitty. Don't give up," the other one says. "We've dressed as ragpickers to blend in," she says to me proudly.

"Excellent disguise," I say. "Let's go." Dolly and I pull the bikes out from underneath the tree canopy, and wave for each of them to get on our bikes. They still look terrified.

"You'll each sit on the seats, and we'll work the pedals," Dolly explains.

"You can hold on to our waists so you don't fall off," I say, sure that I'm strong enough to do this. They get on, and we're off. Dolly and I stand and pump the pedals. She's every bit as strong as I am. I never did this in New York; gave someone a ride on the back of my bike, broke someone free from a hospital! We pick up speed, and the woman holds my waist firmly, hooking her fingers into my belt loops. She cackles with joy like a witch, and I pedal harder and faster to keep up with Dolly. My leg muscles burn but I don't care. I feel a rush in my chest and a surge of freedom for all four of us. We've done it! The sooty night air bleeds into the orange dawn. When we get to Le Monocle, the door is already open and waiting for us.

# LE MONOCLE PARIS

Even though it's six a.m., Le Monocle is packed and dark. It's as if the night never stopped.

"Welcome to the best club in all of Paris!" Dolly sweeps her hand around the room. Butch women in tailored suits clasp the backs of their femme partners on the dance floor. Elegant tables covered in white tablecloths glow with crystal champagne flutes, heavy glass ashtrays, and tumblers full of whiskey. I spot the same cloudy drinks I had at Ma Puce, now in the hands of the best-dressed queers I've ever seen in my life. There's a small jazz band playing in the corner. Aside from the jazz musicians and Dolly, there are no other people of color in the room, and I wonder if that bothers Dolly. The room is loud with music and chatter, warm and welcoming. Women kiss each other openly at the tables, their arms entwined.

"You're finally here!" A woman with short, boyish, blond hair parted on the side, wearing a tuxedo, hugs Dolly and nods at me. I'm not as famous here as I was at Ma Puce, I see.

"This is Lulu. She owns the place," Dolly says, introducing Kitty and her friend.

"Come to the back room," Lulu says, waving us forward and through the dance floor toward a wall covered in photographs of women dancing, riding horses, playing tennis, swimming, doing just about every activity a human could do, but with no cis men. Kitty and her friend keep their heads down, even as the band shifts into a song for them, "On the Sunny Side of the Street."

Dolly pulls us into the back room and the women look shocked by the orgy of it. There are several plush couches and people in various states of undress and lovemaking.

"Let's get you new clothes, clean faces, food, and all of it!" Lulu says, and pulls them deeper into the room and through another door

I didn't notice at first. A Russian doll of a club. Room into room into room. Timeline into timeline into timeline.

"Thank you." Kitty's lover takes my hand and shakes it hard. "We can never repay you. When I looked down and saw your strong shoulders, I felt safe, and then when we got on the bikes, wheeeeee!"

"Oh, it was very easy for me, no problem," I say, and then the two of them and Lulu are gone.

Dolly sits me down onto one of the couches and straddles me. "You were strong and calm. That's sexy to me," she says.

She lifts her skirt and I feel her ass. Round, jiggly. I cup each cheek in my hands. I want to lay her down on her back, spread her legs open, put one hand underneath each perfect half-moon, and lick her until she cries. Button, knob, kitten, lion, venis, junk, bits, jam, pudding. I want to taste salt and piss, make her mound of hair wet with my tongue. I love making people call out with delight. It's my favorite thing, next to turning in my stories and smoking cigarettes. I ignore the gasps around me and put my lips all over her neck and tits. She falls back onto the velvet couch, and opens her legs wide. The vista. The view. The smell. I put my tongue on her until she cries out.

"Yes, everywhere, everywhere." She pulls at the buttons on my shirt and my trouser belt. I look around.

"We're safe here," she says, and slides her hand into my trousers. "Private property."

Her hand makes me come and then I fall backward. Someone passes me a long pipe, which I feel powerless to refuse. I take a long pull and feel deeply tired. My head rolls back against the velvet, which feels like lamb's fur or the inside of my Dolly. I want to see her. I want to lie down next to her and hold her tightly. I want to rest my head on her breasts and sleep until my life here is over and I can go back. My kid is waiting for me. It's time.

# CURES

Dolly nudges me awake. There's light coming in through a small window near the ceiling, the candles have burnt out, and the rest of the couples are gone. "What time is it?" I ask, bodies in a tangle on the couch.

"Come to the front with me. Kitty and Rosalind are going to tell their stories. It's past noon."

The front room is still smoky, but has been rearranged to look more like a meeting house than a bar. There are just a handful of people there, more sober now, present and alert.

Kitty and Rosalind look like they've slept too. They've chosen new clothes. Kitty's in a simple shirt and skirt and Rosalind has chosen woolen pants and a work shirt like I wear.

Lulu's given them drinks and a pack of cigarettes. They sit and eye us all nervously. Kitty's hands shake as she lights a cigarette. After a long drag and exhale, she lights one for Rosalind and begins to speak. Her voice trembles at first and then settles into what she wants to say to us. "In the hospital they hung us by the armpits in slings and our legs dangled in the air. 'We are stones, going nowhere,' I thought to myself some days. 'We are sunk,' I told Rosie here. There were the large rooms and the small rooms. In the large rooms, we ate and slept. Tables and tables and beds and beds. We wore our white starched gowns with the black ribbons tied at the neck and our white caps. We set the table, did laundry, washed dishes, kept house for the biggest house any of us had ever seen, and some of us were rich." She pauses to light another cigarette and take a sip of her drink, which seems to calm her.

"At night, our beds were arranged in tight rows and we tossed and turned," she continues. "We moaned and kicked, farted, sneezed, shit, peed, and bled. There was never any privacy. Sometimes we screamed like infants, the afflicted, the raped, and the cursed. There was a theater of sorts, a place to have your picture taken with the famous doctor. It helped if you let your clothes slide off of your body and you were a good actress. Some of the younger doctors were very handsome, and if you made them happy they would bring you sweets and little bit of fabric or a doll."

Kitty stops and looks down. She squeezes Rosalind's hand. "Now you talk," she says. "Not just me, it can't always be just me."

Rosalind takes her time, finishes her cigarette, lights another. The room grows restless and Dolly goes to the bar and opens more bottles of champagne.

"There are the special small rooms where they take you to suffer. The electricity that will break your teeth. The baths. The mean nurses and the few kind ones. There is a ward where some go and never come back. A dark place, with bars on the doors, the keys to which the meanest nurses keep around their waists. If you stand too close to that door, the nurse will hit you or worse, you'll hear them wailing to be set free. They tie us up, they submerge us, but we are witches and so we float. We have friends, we knit, we pass the time, we draw and write, but mostly we wait." She pauses. "Or rather, we waited."

The room breaks out in applause. Kitty and Rosalind look uncomfortable. Dolly must sense this too because she leads them to a table off to the side with soup and bread for them. They eat and ignore us. Lulu begins what seems to be a meeting about how to close down the hospital. There is a debate about queerness and hospitals that hurts my heart. I overhear one beautiful woman say, "Maybe we *are* sick. Maybe we *do* need to be cured." The room boos and hisses at her.

I find a corner and sink into it. I pull my notebook out of my satchel and start to write, suddenly with full access to both Carley and Charlie. Carley, 2020 Carley, knows the doctor the two women spoke of—he'd become famous for his work at first, and later had to admit that his methods were problematic. My pen dances across the page:

*Hospital, Institution, Orphanage, Wards, Wards of the State, Prison, Prisoners, Patients, and Clients. It is not lost on us that at this time of mass hospitalization and disability, we are terrorizing those seeking asylum more than ever. There is never enough asylum if you do believe in borders. There is no need for asylum if you don't believe in borders.*

*Any port in a storm. Fact. Foxhole. Sanatorium. Body. Infirmary. The dictionary is a comfort and often, I tell my students, a cheat. I do not love definitions at the beginnings of essays. But this is nearly the end and this is a novel.*

*What we fear most is being left in the hospital or of being tricked into staying. We don't mean to spend much time in the hospital and then we die there. The government, through privacy policies, has obscured our viewing of hospital life during COVID. We are not allowed to see the dead and the people working to save the living. Photos are rare and this is intentional. To see would be, perhaps, to know, and then to feel something unimaginable.*

*For years, disabled people were warehoused and locked away. To be unseen, or never seen again. But to have a body is to be disabled. To have a body is to have a medical history. There is no such thing as a preexisting condition. The body is a preexisting condition.*

*In photos, there are large rooms with disabled people milling about, or more formally posed as if to prove they are ladies and gentlemen, upright, and well-behaved.*

*Jean-Martin Charcot, perhaps the most famous neurologist, ran an asylum for hysterics in Belle Époque France called Salpêtrière, which housed some four thousand madwomen. Attempting to provide evidence for hysteria, he employed an artist and a photographer to capture women at the height of their symptoms. The photos were wildly popular. Star patients, like Blanche Wittman, performed for Charcot, often under hypnosis, such acts like barking like a dog and taking off her corset. The sick woman, the asylum became then, sexualized and sensationalized, and mentally ill women vied for Charcot's attention so as to avoid being banished to the incurable parts of the ward.*

*What trauma we enact when we send people away, when we lock them out, when we separate them from ourselves to prove that we are well and safe.*

*I've just met two of these women, and helped them escape. Is it time for me to go home now? I'm thinking of my apartment in Brooklyn, my kid, and my cat. Lana, my bike. A small part of me wants to stay here with Dolly, in this space of resistance, but I'm needed back home too. How I love being two people at once! What power I have! It has been amazing to skip days of medication, but who am I if not made of pills, the present, and the past?*

I stop writing and close my notebook. I smoke a cigarette and listen in as the conversation in Le Monocle grows more heated and circular.

"I'm not gay. I want to live my life as a man, and if I could fully do that, I wouldn't even come here," one says.

"Suit yourself, but we would miss you, Claude."

"I want to live my life free of doctors and surveillance, my parents always watching over me," another person says.

"But if there is a cure for us, why wouldn't we take it?"

"I am not sick."

"You heard Kitty and Rosalind. It was torture there."

Charlie takes over again, though, and has something to say in our Yankee American roughness. "You're all giving me a fucking headache! This is a bar. Get drunk and have fun!"

I stalk into the back room and Lulu calls after me, "How's that book about us coming along?" They all think this is very funny, and I am relieved to have escaped.

# PORTAL 3000

The bar is aflame with heat. There's Dolly opening the front of what looks to be a furnace. I hadn't noticed it until now. She's peering in like Alice down the rabbit hole, and pointing out some features to Kitty and Rosalind.

"If you want to bypass two centuries, you most certainly can. I've heard it's not going to be to great here in Paris for the next twenty years at least."

"But can we come back?"

"I believe so, but nothing is guaranteed at Le Monocle."

My jaw drops and I move closer to get a look.

"You step in, and you're in the year 3000," Dolly explains to me. "It's a portal."

"Why 3000?" I ask.

"It's when things get better or so I've heard," Dolly says.

"We have to wait that long?" I sigh.

"At least the world doesn't end." Dolly is so practical about this portal.

Kitty already has one foot inside the furnace, but Rosalind clings to her arm. "I don't know," she says.

"No doctors from here can get us there," Kitty reasons. "And she says it's good."

Through Kitty's legs, I see a whirling vortex of movement, spinning clockwise, deep purples and pinks, like a child's tunnel on a playground. I crawl down on all fours to get a better look. The color shifts to a pale rose with splotches of deep red as the portal expands and contracts. It reminds me of enthralling and disgusting photos of my own esophagus and colon my doctor once showed me. The insides of us are portals too, I guess.

Kitty steps out of the furnace to whisper-argue with Rosalind.

"I don't want to go in fear," Rosalind says.

"But what do we have here?" Kitty counters.

Dolly and I stare into the roiling sphincter of time. What flashes before us is a slideshow of sorts, a series of happenings, likely dependent on our actions now and in 2020 and beyond. I see boats bobbing in the water holding Pride banners. The city has become water. Then I see a clear spacecraft taking off from a heliport, like Wonder Woman's transparent airplane but bigger. Inside the ship, there are people laughing and dancing. The portal gurgles and I see buildings on fire and an archipelago of mountaintops. The portal burps and sputters and turns to glitter and dust, a glass city built on stilts and cliffs, more animals than people. My last view is something like a club, flashing lights, music, a thumping base, orbs of light, and auras that may or may not be people.

"Would you ever go?" I ask Dolly.

"Me? No, I like it here just fine."

We step back as Kitty and Rosalind step into the furnace. I can't tell if they are happy or sad, more determined to leave than anything else. They wave, we wave back, and that's it. They're gone.

"Dolly," I say. "Thank you. I love you, but I have to get back too."

She's staring at the me that is Charlie/Carley and I know that even if Carley goes, Charlie will stay. She doesn't have to say goodbye, but she does anyway. She gives me a sweet, long kiss and squeezes my ass.

"Orpheus," she says, "don't look back this time."

"I won't."

My walk back through Paris is quick and certain. If I look too hard, I'll want to stay and I can't do that. So I ignore the cafés, ragpickers, street kids, and movie posters. I intentionally blur my eyes—maybe the tears help with this, or maybe I'm not crying at all.

In Charlie's apartment, I open my box of pills and take five or six, a mixture of whatever. I wait to fall asleep and hope for the best. *Pills are a kind of portal too*, I think, as my stomach gurgles to digest them and I drift off.

## REALLY GOOD PANCAKES

I wake back up in 2020, standing, holding Lana, in front of a boarded-up storefront on Nostrand, what was once the entrance to the new Le Monocle. My phone's alarm goes off in my back pocket, the little loopy song that says, *Wake up, it's time to go home.*

I peek through the holes between the slats of the rolled-down gate—an old counter, a refrigerator with its door pulled off, and lots of trash on the floor.

"Was there a club here?" I ask an older man who walks by.

"Club?" he laughs at me, keeps walking, calls back. "A little diner, long ago, but no club. They had really good pancakes."

I get on Lana and ride home. My muscles ache.

I ride back whenever I can, but it's always the shut-down storefront, and never Le Monocle.

## PART 4
## *RESURRECTION*

# DANCE PARTY

For a couple weeks I dream about Paris, and Dolly, and the women from the asylum, and the portals. The maskless world where I got to be free in the midst of months of restriction and confinement. I miss those busy streets and my brief glimpse at a queer world. I wonder what Kitty and Rosalind discovered once they arrived in the year 3000. I hope it was the Pride Boat Parade or the aura dance party and not too much apocalyptic fire. I miss Dolly and I worry about her, but I reassure myself that Charlie is there—my stand-in, my time-avatar, and also a whole other person, who is not me, taking good care.

The Saturday after the election, I deactivate my Twitter account, where I believe I have become the worst version of myself—an addict who scrolls and gets into silly fights, an artist trying too hard to run with the big dogs, a disabled person searching for a dopamine high like the little mouse I named Algernon in high school psychology class and trained to tap a bar for water. I could not stop tapping that bar.

I ride through the park. I stare out over the valley of the big lawn as groups of people dance and sing. Clouds of pot smoke linger just above them. I am so happy I don't know what to do with myself. This is not a familiar feeling but hope, change, release, and joy.

I pedal hard to make it up the hill and to a dance party on a block in Fort Greene. I don't dance really, but I sway and stare and squinch my eyes a lot at the people through my mask as if to say, *I am smiling. I am happy. We voted him out. That fucker. That rapist. Replaced not by my first choice, but still there will be some order, maybe some attention to the law.*

I meet a man in his twenties who is wearing military coveralls, with the top pulled down and tied around his waist.

He wins me over on a stoop where I am sitting to rest. "I like your freckles," he says.

"Thanks. I like your coverall thing," I say, because it's a bold look, very gay, and I don't pick up on the fact that he's hitting on me.

He seems to get that his flirtation is not translating clearly and adds, "I'm Jonah. I'm bisexual."

"Cool," I say. "I'm Orpheus, sometimes called Carley, and I'm bi/pan too. More pan, I guess."

"Do you want to go home with me?" he asks. "Not to be, like, Grindr about it, but why not?"

"This is better than Grindr because we didn't use an app and we're both bi and we located each other without technology."

"Bi power!" He puts out his hand for me to take and I don't ask him about his most recent COVID test or who is in his pod because for one night I would like to not fucking care. I would like to pretend I'm in Paris, and even though I wouldn't have met him at Le Monocle, maybe he would have been one of my fans at Ma Puce.

In the way of Brooklyn panpocalypse and also my '80s teenage small-town life, we ride our bikes to his place.

"I'd like to make references to how dating now is like a Spielberg film, but those will maybe be lost on you," I say at a light while we pause side by side and I lean off of Lana and a little closer to him.

He slides down his mask and it's the first time I see his mouth and chin. He has a devastating blond mustache that is just so McCarren Pool Party that it fills me with nostalgia and longing.

"I watch *Stranger Things*," he says, and slides my mask off my nose and lips.

We kiss at the light and keep riding through the park and into rich-people-brownstone Park Slope.

"You live here?" I ask as we wheel our bikes into the basement of a one of the brownstones that line Ninth Street, the super fancy ones.

"Well, with my parents, but they're out of town."

I blink at him hard because I'm not sure I can do this, but I remind myself that soon he or me is going to peel off those coveralls and hopefully he will be hard forever because #twenties and I can come and come and come.

Later, I am eating out his ass in his way-too-small twin bed while he jerks off and I decide that I was maybe too optimistic about this hookup. But he comes and that in itself is beautiful and pretty. He wants to lick my pussy but I am tired, hungry, and cramped in the bed, so I pull his chin up to my face and say, "Hey, let's have some snacks and take a break?" and he runs down the hallway to the bathroom with the gusto of a lacrosse player on an actual team and I am fine with it, because his ass is so amazing and I bet his parents will have good snacks.

"Yes, BRB, I gotta clean up!"

I put my clothes back on and go downstairs into the gorgeous old kitchen. I'd always wondered what these brownstones looked like—and this one delivers. It's got old-cabinet charm with all-new appliances and stuff galore—stacks of mail, books, plant clippings, and family photos, which I blur my eyes over in order to avoid looking at because I am afraid his mom is my age.

I pull some expensive goat cheese out of the fridge and Jonah is next to me, kissing my neck in a sweet way. "Can I eat this? Do you have crackers?" I ask.

"Yes and yes." He gets crackers for me and heats up something for himself that his mom made.

"Can I show you this movie I love?"

"What is it?" I am focused on getting the goat cheese on a cracker.

"It's called *The Duelists*. It's Ridley Scott's first film," he says.

"Sure." I shrug and shove a cracker into my mouth. "I haven't seen that."

Jonah is giddy and hooks his computer to the TV. What follows is a pretty delightful two hours of Keith Carradine and Harvey Keitel dueling over backdrops that look like Bruegel paintings. There is a beautiful mistress with amazing tits whom we both adore. Jonah and I do a lot of nice smooching, hand-holding, and jokes, and this is the best part of the night for me, which is my constant reminder that often sex is an offering I make to get to intimacy. A barter I wish wasn't always necessary or is perhaps about an old narrative. I must fuck to get this other thing. The transactional mode runs deep in me. I remember my mother bribing my father. Sex for chores.

It has finally come to me who Jonah looks like. "You look like Vronsky in the movie *Anna Karenina*."

"Who?" Jonah knows everything about Russian military history but not so much Russian literature maybe.

"He's a pretty Russian military fuckboy. But I'm not Anna—I mean, I'm not killing myself on railroad tracks."

"Right." He kisses me hard on the lips. "I think it's time for you to go," he says, and I get on my bike and do just that.

Outside, it's so cold and the wind freezes the snot against my nose. I ride the Prospect Park loop alone and wonder how to summon Charlie and go back to Paris where it is probably even colder, but somehow better because it is not now.

As I ride, I think of time as a series of knots I cannot tie. Or the slipknot, at once secure and then pulled taut, not a knot anymore. But a slippery rope. Time is the bad bondage I do, my ties that never keep. There was a man in October I didn't tell you about because Time Passed™. He tied me up well and then didn't listen to the safe word and sweat all over me. When I complained he said, "You are not a devoted enough sub."

"I'm not, now please untie me."

I cried and so he did.

Time has come undone. Time is my body wanting to be untied. Time is shibari knots locked up tight and hidden away. Time shows itself in my body. I do not want to run down the hallway while Jonah looks on. Time is jiggle and bounce, a stomach that is forty-eight is also time because once two babies lived inside of it outside of time, until one was born into time. The park is dark and empty and the naked tree branches cast shadows across Lana and me as we ride the loop. When I first got Lana, when I lived in Manhattan and the pandemic had just begun, I learned to ride the grid of the city, to make a loop out of a square, to set off, to pedal hard, and eventually to return. To be a good parent is to forever return to your child until they are ready to let you go. To be a good girlfriend is to let someone go, or keep them close, depending on what they want. I have found the close and far difficult. As Orpheus, it's my job to play the lute, to write this song in the form of a book, to long for my lovers, and to retrieve them. But many have not wanted to be retrieved or to return to me. This is their right, of course. Lovers are not children. I am not their mother, but oh, how hard it has been for me not to mother my lovers. Every last one of them!

And how lovely it was to be touched! How much I needed to meet Jonah! My hands freeze as I get closer to my apartment. I can't wait to crawl onto my couch and under my comforter.

I try to practice gratitude when I get home and snuggle under my blanket with my cat.

*Accomplishments:*
I have survived (mostly through luck and privilege).
I taught myself to ride the city.
I went back in time and found my way back.
I moved to Brooklyn, where I am happiest.
I wrote this book.
I never did get that improved dictation software, so I typed most of it out. It hurt sometimes. But I am okay.
I learned how to be alone.
I looked back and then forward again.
I saw the future.
I kept my kid alive and helped her with her depression.
I taught when it was almost impossible.

Think of this book as a series of loops. Think of time this way too. Sick time is slower, altered, looped, less fixed, less finite, less able to make its mark on us. If nothing else, we have all had to slow down. Some of us had to stop altogether. Sick time is anti-capitalist, revolutionary if you can accept it or even see it. Care and community in the time of the police state are radical acts. Still, to this day.

Sometimes you move forward with the shitty software. Time is glitch, portal, and pause.

I move from the couch to the bed.

My movement has always been a radical act.

# MUSTACHE POD

Eight months into the pandemic I make a winter pod with Jujubee and a couple—Wolf and Fire—we both trust and love. We agree to test every two weeks before seeing one another and to report our risks to the pod.

On Thanksgiving, Wolf and Fire bring a turkey breast, gluten-free stuffing, and a mixed frozen mezcal drink. I bring an assortment of goat cheeses for the cow's-milk intolerant, which is everyone in the pod.

We get wild at Jujubee's apartment.

"Let's put on lipstick!" she says, and pulls a makeup bag out of the closet. I haven't worn makeup since the lockdown started. I used to love lipstick and mascara, but now it's all pointless, and like many things that no longer seem to be important—hard pants, bright-red lipsticks, a well-manicured pussy, going to an office to work.

"Let's draw mustaches on ourselves!" I actually jump up and down at the thought of it, and I almost pee my pants because I gave birth once and now I have to pee a tiny bit for the rest of my life when I jump, sneeze, or startle.

We crowd around the bathroom mirror. Jujubee paints on our lipstick and I give everyone a special mustache. Mine has a curlicue at the ends, a pencil-thin one. Jujubee gets a bro-ey Williamsburg shaggy one, which she instantly inhabits. Wolf and Fire get handlebars of differing lengths.

We saunter around the apartment with our mustaches and drinks, taking selfies that we don't post because no one is allowed to have joy, especially with a made-up friend pod. Nuclear family pods, yes; but queer alternative family pods, no. Keep it quiet.

I wipe off my mustache before I ride home. It is instinct, I guess. To not cause trouble, even though in the mustache I feel I am my best self, my wittiest, happiest, and most gender-appropriate.

The ride home from Williamsburg to Flatbush is long and flat—through Hasidic Williamsburg, through Bed-Stuy, and then home. The streets are empty in all three parts. It's one in the morning. I miss my kid. I am always missing my kid. When I go out with friends and lovers, like tonight, or write, she's with her dad. This book was written in the half of my life when I don't have my kid. It's because of coparenting that me, a mother in America, with no childcare, can write books. Although lately, because she's almost twelve, she lets me write when she's doing online stuff with her friends. She understands I need to write to be in the world, just like she needs to edit TikToks and make Roblox videos. We give each other this—respect of each other's processes and art forms.

# XMAS EVE

There is a hole in this book called "Time passes."

I joke with Guapo that I've seen other writers do this and I always found it amazing and confident, like swagger for books. So I did it. It's like a magic wand, and depending on the magic show, you go with it or you don't.

Time passes. Part of the semester when I got so busy I couldn't write this anymore. Now that I know there are portals, linear time matters less to me. Writers move in and out of their books, because we must, especially writers with full-time jobs, and isn't that most of us? I also started to write another novel and so I was distracted. And public schools in NYC are shut down, so I spend my weeks when I have my kid trying to keep her on Zoom for six hours straight, which is bananas.

Besides, plot is fake time. Novels speed up, jump around, slow down, zoom in, and zoom out, all for the sake of the story.

During this time hole, I started to date straight cis men again. I remember that I'm bi/pan, and I can date anyone if I like them enough. I go on many socially distant walk dates in the park with them. At first, I worry that I'm not queer enough when I kiss the straight cis men in the park because this is thing that bi/pan people my age often feel or have been made to feel in queer spaces—that we are not enough. But I remember that this is what I do. I am capable of loving all genders and sexualities. What a gift to the world bi/pan people are and still we get so much shit for it, and are very hard on ourselves. Or maybe I am hard on myself like in all things.

I buy my own first vape pen, which my therapist says sounds like an act of independence. I have always smoked other people's pot.

But then also bi men. Jonah. The joy of bi for bi is not to be underestimated.

Jonah and I text about what happened when we met.

"If we meet again, we will have to focus on making me come first," I text.

"Yes, I'm sorry. Absolutely. I got so excited, I think I ran rough-shod over you."

That word. *Roughshod*. Gets me. Pulls me back in. Because it's horses. Trampling. Me into the ground. Forever and ever. Yes, please, I would like to be dead. Some deep subbing desire to be annihilated in the act of serving and also coming.

I have been joking with Guapo that until we get to the vaccine I would like to go into a coma. The vaccine, the vaccine! Who will get it, and when?

I ask Jonah to send me videos of him coming for me, which I adore. There is jizz everywhere and it's all so pretty to me. In one, his long, muscular arm holds the camera so I can see his face, torso, and cock, and with his other hand he jerks off while saying my name, "Orpheus oh Orpheus."

I feel the feeling I have always made fun of in older men, but he is just gorgeous to look at. I feel I could stare at him for hours, and I don't know what to do with this feeling, because once I was a stared-at young person, and now I am definitely not young and considerably less stared at, which I like because I can get more shit done. I bring something else to the table, but what? Daddy vibes. Smarts. Experience. Excellent sexual skills. Communication. GGG. Tits still good. Butt still good. Stomach is another story. Love it as I do, it once held two babies. I want to be all body-positive and mostly I truly love my body, but it is forty-eight and so there are challenges and moments because culture and the patriarchy tell us all day long that we are disgusting and should hide in a cave and die. I refuse this, but I am not immune to it.

I watch that video several times.

"Thank you. I feel competitive now," I text back. "Can I send pics matching your pose wearing my harness and dick?"

"Yes, please!"

I am so grateful for his sweet bi-man energy right now. I hardly ever get to wear my dick. I take off my clothes, step into my silver leather harness, which was a long-ago prescient gift from a straight boyfriend, and slide my blue dick into the hole. The pics turn out really hot. There is something about a woman with a dick that is fire. I send.

"OMG! You're so fucking hot!"

"Thank you!" I lie around on the couch, high from my vape pen, until my hard-on dies, and I find myself cuddling with the cat while wearing a dick. A new moment!

"We should have a porno mag or site called 'Bi Fucks to Give,'" I text.

He "hehhehs" me, and we say good night.

I take off my dick and put it away. It's ten months into the pandemic and I am still desperate for touch. Desperate for someone to sit on the couch with me or sleep in my bed for a whole night. I'm sad that I never get to wear my dick anymore. Eurydice liked the look of it, but we didn't do much with it.

I write this high. I never write high. I think that lately on the apps, I have an invisible sign on my head that says "Will peg you," but then it doesn't pan out or I decide I don't want to because I don't really know the person and it's hard work for me, an act of intimacy I'm not always ready for. Hinge says I live in Little Caribbean, but no one here calls it that. I live in Flatbush between Nostrand and New York Avenues. You can't miss me because I'm right by the hospital.

Go to bed, I tell myself. Dream of another time. Le Monocle. Paris, where you met someone who let you stay the night. Write it all down when you wake up. This book is due in two weeks. What a privilege to have an editor waiting for a book to publish. How lucky you are! Write. Write. Write.

# GPS

Guapo says resolved trauma shuts the time portal. Guapo says portals lead to what you desire but you have to pay a price for it. I am selective about who I tell about the portals. I tell Guapo, of course, because he's heard it all from me. There's nothing I could tell him at this point that would shock him, but mostly I keep it to myself.

On New Year's Day, I watch the Poetry Project New Year's Day Marathon. Everyone is recorded this year, and there's a new wildness to an already wild event. I perform too—my sad suicide poem. I am woman in a leopard-print blazer in front of a Christmas tree, holding her hand out to you. I remember my student from Tanzania who turned her sound way up so that we could hear the frogs in the background of her Zoom. Someone plays old footage of Lewis Warsh and Bernadette Mayer, holding babies and walking around an apartment complex. Long hippie hair, babies and books, wine and words. Poetry is the best genre for having babies, because of the fragment. I could write poems when my kid was a baby, though I had no thoughts then. For novels, I needed half my time back. To make a world, I had to get some world of my own.

My friend Henna won't leave her apartment, and when I text her that I'm worried, she texts back that I'm not listening to her and she won't change her mind. I know how important it is for depressed people to go outside, to be in the world, but am I projecting? I want to help her, but I'm not sure how.

A Christmas tree dies in Brooklyn.

Roaches take over my kitchen.

I read something about the need to manufacture billions of glass vials to hold the vaccine. Corning Glass is part of the push, and I feel some upstate industry pride. We have so little left, but once we had furniture, film, and glass.

I spend my tax money and don't worry much about what will happen when my taxes are due.

The next day I ride Lana to see Picasso, who has decided to go back to Brazil. We meet at our favorite dollar store on Flatbush, which is called 99 Cent Wonders. We haven't been here since before the lockdown. Masked and sweaty in our winter coats, we play a game I invented called "What is this for?" I hold some item up and Picasso riffs on what he will do with it.

I hold up a pack of plastic humping toy animals.

"Butt plugs."

I pull a small saucepan covered in '70s-style mushrooms painted on it off the shelf.

"For brewing ayahuasca."

Glitter pens.

"Ass tattoos."

Dish towels covered in whisks that say "Take a whisk."

"Those are just towels," Picasso says, tired perhaps from packing up his whole life.

The store is pretty empty and we wander the aisles slowly.

"Do you really have to go?" I ask. We haven't seen each other much, but our connection is sweet and fun.

"I'm broke and my family needs me," Picasso says, straightening some loose wineglasses on their shelf.

"I understand, but I hope you can come back."

We've hit the refrigerated section, which scares us both a little. There's some frozen fish and a lot of popsicles.

"I'll be back to do my PhD," he says.

"You got in?!"

"Yes, I'm one of fifteen students," he says, then he surprises me and starts to cry. "It is such a big deal for me, for my family, I don't think you understand where I come from. Me, a trans man from Brazil."

I cry too. My constant empath problem of bursting into tears when anyone else does. "I've never been to Brazil, but I know this is amazing and a very big deal. I wish I could take you to a bar to celebrate."

"There are no bars anymore," Picasso says wistfully. We met at a bar before I even knew I would move to this neighborhood. "I liked this neighborhood because it's busy and full of regular people. You know, workers—like in Brazil, like my family."

"It will be here when you come back," I say.

Outside, the wind whips at our masks and hair. We hug. There's no time to talk about the portals.

"Keep our store in business," Picasso calls back to me as he walks away.

I nod, and my tears stay cold on my face.

# #GAYRIIS

I go to the beach with a new date, a musician named Kite. We talk so much in the car that he can't hear the GPS and gets spectacularly lost, which makes me feel anxious because the drive from my apartment to the beach is a straight shot, Flatbush the whole way.

The tide's going out and the wind is strong at Riis Beach. It's just us and a few other dedicated walkers and their dogs. Sand piles and drifts high along the boardwalk, forming a second wave. We walk from the straight end to the queer end, where I am most at home. Two pairs of pants keep me warm. My date says my long, pink DKNY coat from Burlington Coat Factory makes me look like a popsicle.

I smile real smiles into the wind and let the waves chase me up and down the sand. "I do very much want to be licked," I say.

When we get to #GayRiis, I try to re-create the lying down I did this summer topless. I find my approximate spot and stay in corpse pose for ten full breaths.

There are crab legs that I turn into puppets for goofs. Kite brings me conch shells in his pockets and kisses me. I am not used to this kind of affection. What is a date that lasts a whole day? What is it to be touched and held in a way that isn't about sex or getting someone off?

"How strange that I am a person kissing someone on a beach," I say as the wind whips around us.

"You don't kiss people on beaches? Too cliché for you?" he teases.

"No, it's just that I am usually alone here, or on the straight side with tweens."

He hugs me again. His beard is in my face and I don't mind. It's softer than most beards, and long enough that I can tie it in a knot and yank it hard.

That night I see my friend pod and we eat Indian food and watch a documentary about the Bee Gees. I learn for the first time about how siblings can make a special kind of harmony together that nonsiblings can't, and that a white mob once tried to destroy disco records, which were really all records by Black artists.

How many more white mobs will there be?

The next day, I clean the sand out of the conch shell Kite gave me. There's a stone lodged inside and I'm afraid it's an animal for a moment. I put it down. The stone slides out. Phew. Not a small crab. Not my fellow Cancers taken from their homes.

# QUARANTINE

My phone rings. It's Guapo. "We were exposed," he says, "so she can't come to you. We're going to quarantine for the next week and then get tested."

My worst fear—to get separated from my kid. Every parent's worst fear and the government's glee these last four years. Take children from their parents. Take nursing infants from their mothers. Separate families. Sick time makes so many of us experience the harshness of capitalism. The hospital is a device for separation and for quarantine, and the immigrant taken into custody and put into a cage is made to feel sick, isolated, and alone. Historically, quarantines have often been about race. Detention is the ultimate quarantine. The immigrant labeled as diseased and unallowed to enter the body of the country. Quarantining reminds me of my time in the hospital as a kid, when I felt the most sick and alone.

"But maybe I should still take her?" I plead.

"No, because then all three of us could get sick," he says. He's right, but I don't like it.

"Is this because I have a disability?" I ask.

"You do already have enough to manage," Guapo says. "I don't want you more sick."

I sigh into the phone. "Yes, okay," I say.

"Pauline will go stay at her friend's house. She's going to bring us groceries."

"I'll bring the Nintendo Switch and cookie mix and the children," I say. The children are the special stuffed animals that stay here and sleep in the bed with her. The exalted and chosen babies, the ones I do voices for.

Guapo passes the phone to our kid. "But Mama, how will they talk without you?" It is our one last pretend game. The voices come from my mouth and yet, with the magical realism that is puppetry, she speaks back to them. There is Ma Cherie, the wild French dancer/ semiotician from Paris. There is Basil, the Italian cuddle dragon, who loves to be thrown around while speaking of his special homemade ravioli. There is Ma Terie, an even smaller French cherry, who is also a change purse and very careful with my kid's collected savings. Her voice is so high, I sometimes cough when I speak as her.

"Oh, they will, they don't need me," I lie, and think about the videos I can make and the talking I will do over FaceTime. What is a writer anyway, but a thrower of voices? What is a mother anyway, but a liar?

"Okay," she says, but hers is not the voice of the believer. She is twelve now, and it's panpocalypse. You can't trick these kids. They've been in lockdown for ten months. They know the world is a fucking mess. They have TikTok.

# PAIN POEM

My muscles hurt so much, I cry at night.
I listen to my shell.
Little phone, little sex toy, little ocean.
I fear I could fall in love with a sound artist.
A deejay.
Last night a DJ saved my life.
I score a vaccine appointment.
Is this the end?

I remember that other body I had,
Charlie's/my shoulders were so strong
We used them as a ladder.
In 1935, in Paris, I was not disabled.
I didn't need any pills.
When Dolly and I rode those bikes,
I never sat down, I never wobbled,
And I never fell.

Still, I was me, and she was he.
My therapist once said,
*You've got it all wrong.*
*The pills don't make you into Orpheus*
*You are already Orpheus,*
*Even without the pills.*

I won't look back.
I don't want another self.
I still miss Eurydice,
Though that pang had lessened.
*I am what I am*, like Popeye said.
Just maybe less throb in this shoulder,
Less ache in the stomach, less
Drag in that leg.
But then who would I be?
What would I know?
What could I write to you?

# MIGRAINES, EYE TWITCH, ACCOMMODATIONS

Diagnoses (correct): Dopa-responsive dystonia, depression, anxiety, IBS

Diagnoses (incorrect): Cerebral palsy, Friedreich's ataxia, early onset Parkinson's, multiple personality disorder

Symptoms without medication: can't walk, muscle rigidity (worse on left side than right), hand curling, foot curling, muscle cramping and spasming, can't write or hold utensils, loss of motor skills, pain, pain, pain, suicidal thoughts, suicidal ideation, obsessive thinking, depression, anxiety, neck and back pain, leg pain, constipation, can't sleep, stomach pain, paranoia

Symptoms with medication: muscle pain (especially shoulder neck and legs), heightened stress and exhaustion, tired all the time, slow moving, hyper, constipation, cramps, eye twitches, migraines, muscle spasms and cramps, very reactive, take slights deeply to heart, invent slights, paranoia

Medication: Sinemet 25/100 slow release, Klonopin, Wellbutrin, Lexapro, Omeprazole

Accommodations: None

Another disabled writer and academic whose work and activism I admire posts on social media about how difficult it is when you ask colleagues for accommodations and they act as if you are lazy, difficult, a shirker, someone who is trying to get away with something.

I share my dismay at learning a couple of years ago that, though the students at our university have an office for requesting accommodations and registering their disabilities, faculty and staff do not. Once I asked for my classes to be closer together, so I wouldn't have to walk so far between them. I was told by the Office of Equal Opportunities that it wasn't possible, but asked instead if I would like a motorized wheelchair, which I didn't accept.

There is the rage so many disabled people feel this last year, watching institutions and organizations grant universal accommodations (remote teaching and learning, for example) to entire populations, when for years, we have been told that such accommodations were not possible.

I work hard now at the art of self-accommodation, telling myself that I am modeling for my students healthy ways of viewing disability and being disabled when I rest or cancel an occasional class because of pain, but there are still the voices in my head that tell me I am lazy, a bad professor, that I don't work hard enough. I know this is ideology—our culture's beliefs about illness and disability that we all internalize—but it's a powerful force, like all ideology.

It pains me to write this book.

Even though the university said they'd pay for dictation software, the rigmarole of getting compatible software and getting it paid for was so difficult, I gave up. This is often the way of bureaucracies— add so much red tape, so many forms, so many emails, so much back and forth, that the already tired just give up.

Zoom is a technology that hurts my brain. Its interface. After full days on Zoom, I have migraines and eye twitches. Many abled people do too.

So many workarounds to live, and I've got it easy, I tell myself.

Novels are a work around reality.

# FAT ASS

This week, I feel like I could fall in love because there is a person who is here and who is very nice, funny, smart, and good at sex. Kite is a bi cis man, which is a small quandary I can't explore anymore as a bisexual woman. Do I fear I will lose the essential queer and poly parts of myself if I go with him? Maybe. Yes. Do I always kind of feel there is something missing in every romantic relationship I have? Yes. Because mostly I want a girlfriend and a boyfriend, but I'm too tired and old to manifest that, and maybe the fantasy is better than the reality. I will try to hold on to myself, my core, which is in my chakras, maybe in my ass, the root of me. The performance of my sexuality is a game I'm meant to lose. No matter what happens, Kite is Kite and I am me. Two separate beings in Brooklyn, two single coparents, who do not define each other. Kite has a beard, but remember I have a mustache, even when I'm not wearing it. Here I lay my hand on the codependent's bible, *Codependent No More*, and solemnly swear. I, Orpheus . . .

My body hurts every day, and still I fucked so much these last couple days I hurt my ass and my stomach muscles.

Kite stays overnight and holds me. I'm pretty sure I farted on him and he did not leave. He shook my ass like it was something of value and then I came.

My ass is a part of me that gets a lot of attention. Still pretty round and jiggly, like the kids like it to be. This is my white—Swedish, Cuban, German, English, French? maybe Spanish? ass. I inherited this ass from my father, who inherited from his mother, Eloisa. I have hated this ass and not known what to do with it for many years. I was confused when men followed this ass home and asked me about it. I didn't know what to say because for the longest time I didn't see it or know its power. But I fed this ass well, and eventually I honored it and loved it and in turn it has been loved by many. Two babies lived for a time in the front end of this chassis, and then one died and made a shallow grave there and another lived on and burst forth from me out of a hole not very far from my asshole. I have passed this ass down to my daughter who calls it Cake and likes to shake it when she wakes up in the morning and looks in the mirror. I am so glad she has been released from the shame of having this ass. It took four generations, a cultural sea change, and the good work of so many fat-assed people, but we did it.

# MY KID IS DEPRESSED

I get casual about the roaches, announcing to them before I enter the kitchen that I am coming in: "So please scatter and take your scraps and crumbs to your hiding place." Rarely do they listen, and when they die from the traps or the poison the exterminator lays down from his death tank, they choose the middle of the floor or the next paper towel on the roll. To die in full view is their right, I suppose.

My kid says to me, "I'm losing the best years of my life. I'll never have middle school again," and I can only hug her and make vague promises about eighth grade. "Next fall, it will be normal again. You will finish middle school."

"Will I have cool experiences?" she asks.

"Of course, baby. So many."

"How do you know?"

"Because I know you and I know the world and I'm Mama."

Op-eds warn us that we can never return to normal and that we are wrong to wish for a return to normalcy. I get it. But I just want my kid to go back to school and for me to teach in person again one day.

A couple days later, I see her walking down Flatbush with her best friend. Their heads are pressed together, their coats shrugged off their shoulders, and I'm happy that they have this walk, and each other. Sometimes you don't know you're having a cool experience until it's long since passed. To grow up in New York City is to walk down streets that tourists don't understand or don't even know about, a winter jacket half off of your body like you couldn't care less, even when it's 25 degrees out.

I find that I don't want to stop writing this book. I've turned a draft in to my editor and there are plenty of other things to write, teach, read, and think about, but you are my companion now and I will miss telling you everything.

I stay overnight with Kite and I'm not anxious. I sleep there and wear his T-shirt to bed and sweat on him, and in the morning I go home and feel full and scooped out at the same time. We are having a relationship with feelings, talking, fucking, all of it, and though it is completely foreign to me, I want it. My skin needs touch. I am an animal wandering around looking for another warm animal. He is hairy and willing.

Jonah asks me if I want to see a video of him coming. You see, I'm still poly after all.

"Sure."

"Should I give myself a facial or just see how far I can shoot?"

"Facial," I say, because I'm not sure he can do it. He's gone back to Scotland for graduate school, and the virtual is really all we do except for that first night together, though he often writes to me about the summer and the dates we will have then. I see our WhatsApps as a fantasy portal, a place we both go when we are bored or lonely. He sends me funny YouTube videos, dick pics, and cum shots. I send him my boobs a lot and sometimes my ass in yoga pants.

The laundry spins out in the hallway of my building.

"Can't wait," I add.

"Can I have a pic of your tits?" I lift up my shirt, yank down my bra, and aim. It's not even a very good picture, but nobody cares anymore. I send it, hang up my wet, clean clothes and think about porn, which I never really watch unless someone asks me to watch it with them. Because I'm such a novice to it, I usually ruin it for the other person by getting too worked up by the actual skills of porn actors. It's impossible for me to fathom how that big of a dick can go in that asshole, or how long those two women can eat each other out, and so I rave.

The ping of WhatsApp. I watch. He says, "And now I will attempt to come on my own face," and then he smiles at the camera—at me, whoever else this may go to.

"Oh fuck," he says, rubbing the tip of his cock hard like I know, from other videos and not so much in person, that he likes. And there it is, the cum shot, and it shoots up and hits him in the face and he moans and really I squeal because he's so cute and talented and it is hard to do that. Who has that much cum?

"Amazing," I text. "You should be a porn star."

"Hahahaha."

"Good job!"

"Thank you!"

Such is the nature of our chats, though sometimes we go off on bi things and how nobody believes in bisexuality and also how cats are better than dogs. He is also a good source for lesser-known government bullshit and COVID lore because he's a dork, as he says. I'm not horny about the video, but it did cheer me up and drag me away from obsessing about Kite, who has a difficult Baby Mama who I fear needs him far more than I do. I don't need anyone! At least that's what I tell myself.

Jonah got me through the deadly hours between four and five p.m. when the sun sets and it all seems hopeless and I wonder, just like my kid does, if I will ever have any cool experiences again.

I have to make one syllabus from scratch and decide not to change the other one at all, except for the due dates.

In my program, as contract faculty, most of what I do is train myself to teach new courses every semester that require whole new sets of readings, assignments, lesson plans. I do this because I get bored, but it's also the nature of our program, which is interdisciplinary, and lets students cook up whatever project they like. It's cool, I swear, but also, we are very tired.

I said, *We are all very tired.*

# CODE

At first, the vaccination line doesn't move because there's a glitch in the computer system.

I drop my phone on the sidewalk and the screen cracks spectacularly. Again. When I try to scroll, tiny pieces of glass needle my finger.

Volunteers bring people with canes and walkers to the front.

Soon, I am inside the school. I see the metal detector and a trophy case. Step up six feet, wait, step up six feet, wait, step up six feet, wait.

"At this site today, we will vaccinate 2,500 people," a police officer tells the line.

"Thank you," I say, though I can't remember the last time I thanked a cop.

When I get to my station in the cafeteria, there's a woman in yellow scrubs and two masks.

"Go ahead and fill this out," she slides the small white vaccine card to me, and I do.

"Are you left-handed or right-handed?"

"Right."

I take off my coat. There's the small, hard pinch on my left shoulder, then a Band-Aid.

"Thank you for taking care of us," I say, and follow the volunteers waving us into the high school's auditorium, where we all sit for fifteen minutes before we are allowed to go.

Back outside, the line is a square around the fence, but it keeps moving. The virus is inside me now, teaching my cells a code or a hack I will likely never understand.

As I walk toward Lana, I see Eurydice up ahead. I want to turn around and run, but it's too late. She sees me and waves timidly. She's alone, no Hera this time, and standing at the back of the vaccination line.

I take a deep breath and walk toward her, though every atom in me wants to run and implode or disappear into vapor or mist. Instead, I decide to tell her what happened to me that night.

"Hey," I say. "You got an appointment too."

"Yeah, I did, but not Hera."

"That sucks."

"She's mad at me for not booking an appointment for her too."

I nod like I care about their relationship drama, but also that feels like something familiar that Eurydice would do. I feel a small twinge of relief that we are not together. The first! I am healing, I think. From her, from how COVID has changed me. Not healing so much as accepting that I have changed, we are all forever changed.

Eurydice gives me a look I can't quite interpret. She's dressed like a skater girl, with a little hat on the back of her head, and a short, puffy winter jacket. Maybe she will always be the cutest to me.

"I met someone and I went back in time to Paris, to the original Le Monocle, and I became this other person, Charlie. We rescued two women from an asylum and I saw a portal into the future too. I also kind of had a new girlfriend there, Dolly." I pause.

Eurydice's eyes widen and I know she thinks I've lost it. Maybe I have lost it, but haven't we all? Aren't we all entitled to fall apart and break down sometimes? To escape to other landscapes, histories, and people.

"Babe," she says, putting her hand on my shoulder. "Are you okay? Do you want to come over and have Hera and I make you dinner?"

I still love it when she calls me babe. I let her rest her hand on my shoulder because it feels nice and it's her, Eurydice, the first woman I ever fell in love with, the one my stupid then-boyfriend said "made me gay." She didn't do that, I was already queer, but I needed a push out of the closet, and she was there for that. She never flinched and in the time we had, she loved me hard.

"Can we hug?" I ask. "Like, for closure."

"Sure, but I'm not vaccinated yet," she says.

"But I am, or at least partially," I say, shrugging my shoulders. After so long, but so quickly, really, we have a vaccine. "Besides, we have to take risks, right?"

She pulls me into her puffer jacket and squeezes me tight. We let our whole bodies come together, and I smell her conditioner and skin cream. I squeeze her back.

"I'm dating a bi dude," I say. I feel like telling her I'm not single.

"That's good, sometimes dudes are fun," she says, and then she lets me go. "You really should come and eat with us. You can bring your guy."

"Okay, maybe," I say. "I hope the line goes quickly for you," I add, then walk away. This time, I don't turn around.

On a different street, I cry under a tree and stare up at the bare branches and the gray January sky. I am a person full of the pharmacy and now a little bit of COVID. Made into myself by pills, and full of despair, hope, shit, blood, and guts. I have said goodbye to Eurydice. It felt good to hug her, and to get something like closure with her. Maybe I will have dinner with her, maybe I won't. I don't have to decide anything now.

I find Lana, unlock her, and ride from Canarsie back to Flatbush. I don't look back because Thoreau said not to, unless you are planning on going that way, which I wasn't.

# SKETCHES

I can't watch the trial, but I read about it every day and look especially closely at the sketches. Courtroom drawings and sketches remain a vestige of art and art-making in an otherwise procedural institution. The courts. The carceral state. The system of accountability, if there is any. But the drawings convey something else. I stare for a long time at the one of the cashier, a nineteen-year-old Black man named Christopher Martin, who accepted the allegedly counterfeit twenty-dollar bill from George Floyd. His manager told another worker to call the police. Martin describes the guilt he still feels. I keep return-ing to this sketch, drawn by longtime court artist Jane Rosenberg, which she does in pastels—mostly black, brown, white, and hints of blue. She captures that guilt and anguish. I think, too, of Darnella Frazier, who took the video that likely made the conviction of Derek Chauvin possible, and her feeling that she didn't do enough to help George Floyd. There's also Rosenberg's drawing of George Floyd in the convenience store, made possible through Martin's recollections and store footage—he is tall and strong, holding his money, wearing a black tank top, black pants, and black sneakers. There are touches of blue in the store too, but they are light, perfectly placed.

The blues in all of this last year, and in all of the protests we attended last summer. The blues as Black vernacular form. The blues as a form of witnessing. The ever-increasing amount of brutality we must protest. The violence of white supremacy and how it hopes you will close your eyes and turn away. How the video, the sketch, the word, and the song are records against turning away.

In this book and in this last year I have tried to stay present, to not turn away.

# DÉNOUEMENT

I am obsessing over the line, "I use the little goldy pencil," from *Baby Precious Always Shines: Selected Letters Between Gertrude Stein and Alice B. Toklas.* This is the only gift Eurydice ever gave me and sometimes I take it down from the shelf and wonder what it would have been like to have a wife. Me, the author of a novel called *The Not Wives,* longing for a wife. I don't much want to be a wife, but sometimes I'm curious about having one.

I use my little goldy pencil to get through the days of the long winter. I use it to teach, write, and mark up the books I teach. I take good care of the kid and the cat. I try, I do. I water my plants, vacuum, sweep up the roach carcasses, change the kitty litter, teach my classes, pay my bills, wash the clothes, go to the grocery store, clean the toilet—the mundane tasks of adulthood, some would say straight wifedom. But I'm not a wife.

Mostly I write with the goldy mechanical pencils and marker pens in my big notebooks with no lines in them. When I was getting my master's in creative writing, I made a certain very famous older male poet, beloved by many but not by me, very angry with my overuse of gerunds. I am reclaiming them now. Forever and ever. Becoming. Being. Waiting. Molting. Shifting. Doing. The gerund is a domestic form, a feminine ongoingness perhaps. It refuses to transmit a start and a stop. *The pandemic was ongoing and never-ending, it seemed to her that winter. She did the planting and the sewing. Hers was a life of doing.*

My writing has always been obsessive, recursive, ongoing, every day. The initial name for my disease was dystonia with diurnal fluctuations. *Diurnal* means "daily" or "of each day." My writing is diurnal too.

I am writing with my little goldy pencil.

I was writing with my little goldy pencil.

I will be writing with my little goldy pencil.

I will be writing with my little goldy pencil until I die.

I am longing for the cicadas to come and overwhelm us with song. Brood X will be one of the largest broods in history. They will be singing for two weeks.

Kite is staying inside because he is so depressed. I am finding a therapist for him. Jonah is flying back to New York City. Picasso is asking me if I want to go to Mexico with him, so he can have company for the waiting period to get back into America. My kid was standing in line for her first shot and then she got it. Some of the mothers were crying.

I am using my little goldy pencil to fix this book.

Picasso texts me that autofiction and fiction can be theory—"The best kind," he writes. I forget this sometimes. This book has its theories, both in plain sight and hidden. I am leaving them for you to figure out.

It may be that as a young girl who couldn't walk, I became adept at witnessing and watching. I've had to train myself into action and out of silence, literally to move forward. If able-bodied narratives have movement—Aristotelian arcs, male climaxes and releases, dénouement, as my wonderful editor says, then what does a disabled narrative have?

Rests, naps, wanderings, stillness, witnessing, waiting, rigidity, pain, and action—but on their own terms. I bought Lana to force myself to move. The bicycle is a plot device.

*Dénouement* is French for "untie." To untie is so much messier than to resolve, to seek resolution. It defies conclusion and ending completely. To untie a bow on a present is to release a gift. To untie a shoe is to let a foot out. To loosen a necktie is to let its wearer breathe.

So many strictures in this country and in abled-narrative forms.

I am not making any pretty bows. I am only untying them.

# ACKNOWLEDGMENTS

First of all, thank you to Feminist Press for listening to my wild idea to serialize the first half of a novel during a pandemic, and saying YES. Jamia Wilson, former executive director and publisher; Lauren Rosemary Hook, interim director; and Lucia Brown, external relations manager, all brought such vision and excitement to the first wave of this book. Big thanks to Neeti Banerji for her tender and illuminating illustrations. For all of you who read along online and wrote to me to tell me to keep going, I appreciate you so much.

After those first eighty pages got serialized, there was the whole rest of the book to write. I want to thank my editor at Feminist Press, Nick Whitney, for helping me shape a mess of a draft into a book. Nick's kindness, intelligence, insight, wild ideas about time travel and portals, and beautiful shirts helped me through several big and necessary revisions. I couldn't have finished this book without Nick, and I hope everyone gets to work with editors and staff as fun, creative, and adventurous as the team at Feminist Press.

Suki Boynton made me a second wonderful cover for this book. Thank you, Suki, for your beautiful designs and for putting torn paper on the covers of both novels. Thank you Jisu Kim for publicity and Drew Stevens for typesetting. Thanks to the rest of the FP team, including Rachel Page and Isla Ng.

Thank you to Michelle Tea for creating Amethyst Editions and championing queer stories that are not just about coming out.

My writing group—Lynn Melnick and James Polchin—read and gave me feedback on many pieces and parts of this book, as well as sustained me through some dark COVID thoughts. Matt Longabucco reads everything I write, and I'm incredibly lucky for that.

For some of the information about the neurologist Jean-Martin Charcot, I am grateful for the article "In Search of Hysteria: The Man

Who Thought He Could Define Madness" by Allan H. Ropper and Brian Burrell, published on LitHub on September 20, 2019.

COVID hit some communities harder than others, and as a single, queer, disabled person, I often feared I might die from loneliness. Thank you to the people who made pods with me, got tested with me every two weeks, and knew that the nuclear straight family is not the only way to make a unit. My first pod was Matt Longabucco and Rachel Valinsky. We coparent a child together so this was inevitable, but still Matt and Rachel hugged me a lot, brought me food, drove me to Brooklyn, and celebrated my birthday with me, all during lockdown. Thank you to my second pod, Jem Bywater, Rob Bywater, Willa Bywater, Arielle Simone, and Mike Simone. When Malka and I visited during lockdown, we were broken and sad, and you helped us feel loved and nourished again. Thank you to my third pod, Elke Dehner, Joelle Hann, and Jason Nunes. Pod life forever! We did it! We made it through the final stretch with dance parties, lots of food and drinks, tarot, pillows, and sleep!

Thank you to Philip William Stover for calling me several times a week and being so hilarious and present. You make so many books possible, and you don't even know it.

Thank you to Madeleine George and Lisa Kron for surprise boosts, moving help, deep friendship, radical goddess-momming, and support that made it possible for me to finish this book.

Thank you to Amy Shearn for welcoming me back to Brooklyn with Terrace Talks and special cocktails.

I have so many great friends, colleagues, and artists who love and sustain me. Thank you to Alex Baker, Beka Chase, Martha Conner-Vandyke, Adjua Greaves, Stephanie Hopkins, Karen Lepri, Brendan Lorber, Bill Martin, Tracey McTague, Suzanne Menghraj, Jonna Perrillo, Sejal Shah, Kaia Shivers, Smoota, Amy Touchette, Joe Vallese, Nicole Wallack, and William Webb. If I forgot anyone, I'm sorry. I'm old!

Thank you to Keith Fullerton Whitman for new love and getting back on Hinge that one day. You are a very good Daddy. Thank you to sweet Calder for your five-year-old joy.

Thank you to Alejandra, Ben, and Miro.

Thank you to my students, who had such a miserable year and did it all with so much grace and humor.

Lastly, thank you to my kid, Malka, who makes me laugh every day, watches queer TV with me, shows me TikToks, and is the wisest one ever.

## Other Amethyst Editions
## at the Feminist Press

Amethyst Editions is an imprint founded by Michelle Tea championing emerging queer writers who complicate the conversation around LGBTQ+ experiences beyond a coming-out narrative.

**Against Memoir: Complaints, Confessions & Criticisms**
by Michelle Tea

**Black Wave** by Michelle Tea

**Fiebre Tropical** by Julián Delgado Lopera

**Margaret and the Mystery of the Missing Body**
by Megan Milks

**The Not Wives** by Carley Moore

**Original Plumbing: The Best of Ten Years of Trans Male Culture**
edited by Amos Mac and Rocco Kayiatos

**Since I Laid My Burden Down** by Brontez Purnell

**Skye Papers** by Jamika Ajalon

**The Summer of Dead Birds** by Ali Liebegott

**Tabitha and Magoo Dress Up Too** by Michelle Tea,
illustrated by Ellis van der Does

**We Were Witches** by Ariel Gore

amethyst editions

The Feminist Press publishes books that ignite movements and social transformation. Celebrating our legacy, we lift up insurgent and marginalized voices from around the world to build a more just future.

See our complete list of books at
**feministpress.org**

**THE FEMINIST PRESS**
AT THE CITY UNIVERSITY OF NEW YORK
**FEMINISTPRESS.ORG**